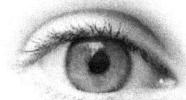

Somebody Came

It is a shock to Seph when she meets her childhood playmate again but, like so many things in her life, she tackles problems head on. For any Girl Friday, impossible situations are normal and meeting her brother, again, after all these years is just amazing... especially as he is dead... Unfortunately, her fun-loving brother likes to meddle in everything. So, the big questions are – will she ever meet someone special who won't mind her brother coming on dates? Will Dion ever tire of involving her in trying to solve crimes? And, more importantly, should she tell her parents?

First published in Great Britain in 2019 by U P Publications Registered Office: St George's House, George St, Huntingdon, Cambs, PE29 3GH

Cover design copyright © U P Publications 2019

Copyright © Mai Griffin 2019

Mai Griffin has asserted her moral rights

A CIP Catalogue record of this book is available from the British Library

This edition ISBN 978-1-912777-02-0

eBook ISBN 978-1-912777-03-7

FIRST PAPERBACK EDITION

Published by U P Publications

www.uppbooks.com
www.maiwriting.com
www.maigriffin.com

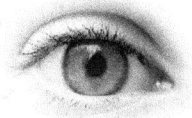
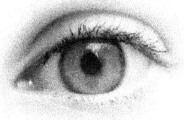

by Mai Griffin

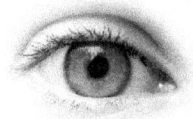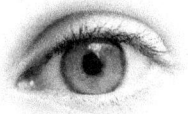

Somebody Came

Mai Griffin

U P Publications
2019

Although the characters are fictitious, my daughter, to whom this book is dedicated, might enjoy being reminded of actual incidents.

Mai Griffin 2019

For Gaile

Somebody Came

At sixteen years old, my sight returned...
Oh no, that could be misleading...

Writing her autobiography was not going to be as easy as she'd expected. She would be twenty-three soon and the story of her life, which she'd started writing on her eighteenth birthday, had dried up before filling twenty pages. She'd soon got used to seeing things that others couldn't, and after a while it wasn't a novelty any more.

The manuscript, buried in a shoebox at the back of her wardrobe and found whilst sorting out old clothes for a car boot sale, had fuelled her sudden, fresh enthusiasm to update the story. Already she was facing hurdles. Perhaps *second sight* would be better than *sight* or maybe *insight.* On the other hand, something seen before it happened, must be *foresight...*

She sighed heavily.

If she struggled over every word it would never be finished and there was no time to write more now anyway!

Staring out of her bedroom window at the sunlit garden below, she wished she hadn't let her mother see her writing so often in her notebook. Her mother, curious to know what she was writing about and commenting with pleasure on her enthusiasm, had pushed her into admitting what she was doing. Telling her was a big mistake.

She should never have said that she was going to write down every single thing she could remember, because interested queries about where she was up to, were off-putting (and probably the reason she'd dried up in the first place).

Questions about whether it was up-to-date and, "When will I be allowed to read it," stopped long ago, when Seph pleaded for no peeking and promised that her mother would be the first to see it.

Now that five years had gone by, and she had so much more to record, maybe it was safe to resume writing.

Her mother had given up asking about it ages ago and her *'life-so-far'* story was probably forgotten so Seph was hopeful that her scribblings would be safe from scrutiny. Her bedroom was large enough to include an office desk, and she knew her mother would never dream of looking through that.

Deciding where to start was not difficult because until she was three years old, her life was happy and uneventful but, after that…

Re-reading the first few pages of her happy, far from lonely, childhood memories, Seph could picture her mother's incredulity if, and when she did eventually get to see it.

The idea of adding to her first twenty pages seemed like a good idea but it would never have occurred to her to write anything at all had she not seen the boy again, in the garden, seven years ago.

She'd always loved the view from her bedroom window, whatever the time of day or the weather but, on that special day, something startled her. A strange figure was near the rockery. When first glimpsed, he'd looked exactly like the little boy who had always been around to play with her, when she was little. He'd been about her age - they were both just kids who laughed together a lot... She now had no idea what they'd found so funny, but her memories of him were all good.

There surely must have been a day when she'd noticed he wasn't about and missed him, but she'd never questioned his presence or absence. Then the excitement of moving to another country for three years drove her playmate from her mind. After all, going abroad meant that she had to say goodbye to all her other friends, so why would he be different?

Living near other army families, as they moved with her father's job, meant she was never short of new playfellows, so she didn't give him another thought until she was twelve. Then, one day she overheard her mother telling a friend about being aware of another child laughing with three-year-old Seph, in the garden. Curious to see who it was and wondering how they had managed to get in, she had taken a couple of drinks outside. Seph was still laughing, although she was apparently playing alone.

Seph knew that her mother was wrong, she hadn't been alone. The boy had been real enough to Seph and she wondered who he could have been and what had happened to drive him away.

She knew that she was her parents' second child and, overhearing them one day, she learned that she often appeared to be laughing with a companion and they liked to think it was her brother, only a year older, had he lived. They wanted to believe that Dion, in spirit, was returning to play with her.

Thinking back to that conversation, she recalled the thrill of realising that her little playmate had probably been a ghost – and not just any ordinary ghost, he might have been her brother!

It was a shock seeing him again on her sixteenth birthday, staring up at her from the garden below, where they'd played so happily – literally, a ghost from her past.

As she watched the small boy, her astonishment grew. He laughed and waved to her and, when she waved back, he grinned a familiar smile at her as he started to shimmer in and out of focus, changing very slowly until, in the space of a few minutes, he'd grown into a tall, handsome teenage boy, the image of her father, when he was young.

She didn't rush to tell her mother that she'd seen Dion, the little boy, again; it felt like something private, a precious gift that she might lose by sharing. Her ability to see him had returned and until she understood more about why he went away and why he came back, she decided that she would never talk about him.

So, after a thirteen-year gap, he'd returned, and she knew, without a shadow of doubt, that he certainly was her brother. The question was, why had the ability to see and hear Dion ever left her?

Now, another seven years on, she had lost her fear that he might disappear and realised that he was just as mystified by the situation as she was herself.

If either wanted to talk, they had only to wait at the rockery and the other would soon come. As the years passed, their confidence grew. Wherever she was, Seph had only to think of him and he would appear. Whatever she was enjoying she liked to share with him, whether it was a film or a party.

He needed to learn about life, and she wanted to help.

All in a Day's Work

The years since his return had been fantastic; she couldn't imagine life without him and didn't want to tempt fate by revealing his presence. She was, therefore, determined to record everything she could remember. Not only would she enjoy reliving the adventures they'd shared but one day, more importantly, they would bring joy to her parents.

It wasn't as if there was much time free to write, anyway.

Until she started her promised job (the contract was signed but the position wouldn't be vacant until September) Seph was freelancing as a 'girl Friday' – ready to tackle anything legal for a fee.

Dog-walking was her favourite job and anything to do with housework was her worst nightmare but the chore that had worried her the most, so far, was cooking a meal for five of her father's business colleagues when her mother was ill, even though the food was already prepared.

After a successful evening, when the guests learned of her 'Girl Friday' scheme, they became some of her best customers. Two of the diners immediately booked dates for her to cook for them.

Another said she would be a gift from the Gods if she could get along with his eighty-year-old mother who was now a permanent fixture in his home. Although his mother insisted that he and his wife could leave her alone and enjoy their social life normally, it was impossible.

The first time they tried, she'd left a frying pan full of cooking oil over a full flame on the gas stove, because she suddenly fancied bacon and eggs, and then abandoned it to answer the 'phone in the sitting room, which was pointless anyway, as she was hard of hearing.

The bacon, half-unwrapped, was too near the stove – the paper became hot and burst into flame, setting fire to the oil in the pan... Riveted to her favourite television show, with the volume turned to maximum, she failed to hear the smoke alarm. Fortunately, a neighbour did and, when ringing the doorbell brought no response, he'd called the fire brigade!

After a few more near disasters, they'd accepted a friend's offer to sit with her. His mother protested bitterly; her entire evening would be ruined. Instead of being able to enjoy peace and quiet, she'd have to entertain somebody.

Afterwards, she grumbled irritably for days. Apparently, having settled down at last with coffee and crisps, the woman talked all the way through 'Strictly Come Dancing' and her boring opinions drowned those of the experts. As if criticising the dresses wasn't irksome enough, she boasted endlessly about the wonderful costumes her own mother used to make for her, when she tap-danced as a child.

Worn down by his mother's complaints they gave in to her desire to be left alone and, after extracting a promise that she would not cook while they were out, they went to a local concert. Returning, three hours later, they found her on the floor with a broken ankle; she had climbed a kitchen step-stool to reach a book from the top shelf in their study.

Seph would be the third person they had engaged since the fall, so the ankle was better now, unlike his mother's attitude towards her sitters.

Babies were well within Seph's scope and children were manageable because she enjoyed playing games with them, if all else failed, but caring for an adult was something new and she was a little nervous. She glanced at the clock and put the manuscript on the table next to her bed – maybe she would add something before sleeping, later. She had over an hour to make herself look like a reliable and responsible granny-sitter.

The day before, in preparation for the challenge, Seph had checked the TV schedules so that she could appear knowledgeable about whatever was showing and had immersed herself in borrowed magazines on cooking and parenting. She would produce them to help conversation, if necessary – she did not, after all, expect to have much in common with an elderly grandmother.

In record time, with still thirty minutes to spare before she had to go out, she was showered dressed and ready, except for dabbing on some makeup. After shoving her discarded clothes in the laundry bin, ready for the washing machine, she reached for her book again, rummaged in her purse for a pen and stared, purposefully, at a blank page.

Lost and Found

Glancing briefly at her watch, Seph started to write...

Unable to move away from the window, or take my eyes off him, in case he faded away, I just stared at him until he beckoned to me.

It was obvious that I couldn't stand there forever, so I tore myself away from the window and dashed downstairs.

I can't recall everything we said, or even if we spoke aloud at all – we just seemed to communicate as if we'd known each other all our lives, which I suppose we had, in a funny sort of way.

He said he'd been shocked when he visited the garden and I wasn't there.

I asked why he didn't come after us – after all, being a ghost, he had no bags to pack or tickets to buy.

I know, now, that I was the one who went away.

Our house was empty for ages, when my soldier-dad was posted abroad. As a captain, there was a quarter waiting to house us all and we were excited to be moving to Singapore.

Dion said, if he'd known I was going he would have stuck close to me and I wouldn't have got lost. He ignored me when I pointed out that he was the lost soul, not me!

I asked why it had taken him so long to find me again and he supposed that, at first, Grandma had given him things to occupy his mind.

Later, as he grew up, he was busy with real jobs.

Having returned to earth eventually, and seen that we'd returned, he had lingered patiently in the garden for a long time ...waiting for me to look out of my window.

Although he had grown up in spirit, he kept returning to the garden as a child, sure that I would remember him and be better able to accept him as an adult...

The shrill sound of the telephone in the hall didn't disturb her, but when her mother shouted that she had to leave straight away, she glanced at the clock ...surely not, it was nowhere near the time she had been given.

It seemed that her client and his wife had to leave earlier than planned and his mother was now alone and expecting her.

Just as she was in full flow!

Hopefully she wouldn't forget what she was about to write... Thank goodness she was nearly ready to go out.

Now she had real work to do: time to put her journal aside again. She put it under her pillow, out of sight, then dashed downstairs, shouting a hasty farewell to her parents. Outside, she grinned as she saw that Dion was already in the passenger seat of her car.

As she drove away, Seph thought of all he had told her about their Grandma, Dad's mother, the one she had never known. She felt sad and wondered why Grandma and Granddad didn't come to visit her as well.

There was still so much to discover about her brother's world but writing down what she had learned, so far, would keep her busy enough.

She was fascinated by the things Dion had already done and now that he was trusting her to help him, there was no danger of running out of material!

Dion, at four-years-old, had been upset when, day after day he came to the garden and she never came out to play. She once pointed out that, if he'd gone inside to look for her, he would have seen that it was empty. He looked shocked and said he could never have done that.

She'd asked, why, and his answer was funny, but quite reassuring...

Perhaps she could put that in somewhere... if anyone ever did read her story, it was something they would probably like to know.

Anyway, diary addition and omission decisions must wait for now.

Her little Mini made good time; the house was in sight ...at least she thought it was the right house...

Why was there a small excited crowd gathered round the front door?

Well, it promises to be anything but a boring evening, Seph thought, intrigued, despite her nervousness. Slowing down almost to a stop, she turned into the driveway and parked, as instructed, under a small carport.

Her arrival had not gone unnoticed...

Granny Sitting

As she walked from the corner of the house, towards the crowd surrounding the front door, several people detached themselves from the main group and surged towards Seph. All but one were clutching collecting boxes. The shortest man was the most talkative, with by far the loudest voice. He could even be heard above the wailing of a colourfully clad woman who was clearly distressed, apparently about being the only one empty-handed.

When 'Mr Chatty', the obvious leader of the group, demanded that they should let him handle the matter, they fell silent and let him speak. He explained that he was across the road when he saw Mr and Mrs Mather drive away and, within minutes, he saw Fatima ringing their bell. He turned, indicating the tiny woman, whose wails grew louder when she heard her name.

The others rallied round Fatima and did everything but clap a hand over her mouth, while their spokesman continued. "I would have stopped her from calling here had I been able, because I guessed that Mrs Mather senior must be alone, and she is, to say the least, unpredictable. Can you help please?"

It took quite a while to grasp the whole story because of Fatima's constant interruptions, but finally the story emerged.

Earlier, when politely invited by Fatima to contribute to a local charity, Mrs Mather had nodded and left her at the door. Returning with a twenty-pound note she had started to put it into the slotted tin but suddenly drew back and asked how she could be sure that the charity was legitimate.

Fatima, an immigrant, took this as throwing doubt on her own legal position and had produced her precious folder, which she carried everywhere in a holdall. 'The Ancient one', as Fatima kept calling her, seized it and ran inside, slamming the door (or 'slumming my face' as Fatima shrieked... 'Taking money too').

This latter information seemed to annoy the rest of the collectors far more than the other charges, as if the potentially generous Ancient had stolen it from the tin!

Eventually, Seph felt she knew enough to try communicating with the unresponsive Mrs Mather.

While she was wondering how to start – after all, this was happening on her watch and she had to prove she could cope – Dion suddenly materialised grinning from ear to ear, holding his sides, laughing.

Really, Seph thought, his sense of humour is so childish – but then, he hadn't grown up with adults; he didn't have a chance to grow up at all, she reflected, feeling suddenly mean.

Dion pointed at the house and disappeared but, in a flash, Seph knew she had to act.

She couldn't handle the situation from outside – she had to get in.

He was the best – nudging her in the right direction – brilliant, if it worked.

Shouting through the letterbox, she called to Mrs Mather and asked her to open the door.

"I am Persephone Montague, you are

expecting me. I'm looking forward to meeting you." Within a few seconds, a stern voice demanded that everyone else should move away to the gate, so Seph shrugged an apology to the group and asked them to be patient; she would return in a few minutes.

Inside, with no formal greeting, Seph was ushered from the spacious entrance hall by her hostess/charge to a dining room, where the table was covered with official-looking papers. When Seph could pull her eyes away from the distracting, extravagant décor – and oil paintings – to the open folder, she saw that uppermost was a letter from the National Asylum Support Service, NASS, and an ID with a photograph; it was of Fatima. The letter instructed that asylum seekers should always carry them everywhere. No wonder the poor girl was manic.

"Mrs Mathers, may I ask why you took these from the collector at the door?" Seph asked hopefully.

For all she knew, Mrs M senior might, in her eighties, be completely gaga and beyond thinking clearly about why she did anything!

"Before we go into that, we have to sort ourselves out," came the reply. "Call me Grace – Mrs Mathers is James's wife. The name you shouted through my letterbox was much longer than the one I expected. I hope you're not an imposter!" Upon hearing that Seph was indeed Seph, Grace relaxed and indicated that they should pull out two dining chairs.

Piling the papers together with great care to keep them straight, the rather stately-looking, silver-haired woman quite clearly felt justified in having taken them. "It suddenly struck me that I was handing money over to a charity I'd never heard of and I wanted to ring someone to check. I thought the girl was telling me that it was legal and that the proof was inside the folder."

The exiled collectors at the end of the driveway were now talking loudly, staring worriedly at the closed front door and one held a cell phone to his ear. Excusing herself quickly, Seph pulled the curtain aside and gave them a thumbs-up to show she was okay and had not been axed by a madwoman.

Grace carried on with scarcely a pause...

"I've heard about strangers tricking their way into houses, so I took it quickly and shut the door before she could follow me. I intended to phone a JP I know, but I saw that small, round fellow come into the garden with a similar tin and I recognised him straight away – he has visited my son here on business, several times, so I knew it must be OK. Then I started nosing through the paperwork – fascinating!"

Seph reminded her that the charity workers were waiting for the return of the folder. They were so upset that it might be a good idea, she suggested, to invite them all in for a cup of tea and maybe to put her donation into Fatima's tin.

Grace liked the idea and shooed Seph out, but called after her, "Make it coffee, I don't do tea – there's wine too, if someone can open the bottle. I was never any good at screwing corks..."

Aftermath

An hour – and several bottles of wine later – Grace and Seph were alone. The two men and three women, who had initially been wary about accepting an invitation to enter the house, departed with much hand-shaking and flushed with success. Fatima was clutching her precious folder and the promised note had joined the donations already rattling in her tin...

Although her tears had dried, she looked a little dazed and she had hiccups. Seph knew she had asked for 'toning water' but, by mistake, had probably picked up a drink with gin in it ...most likely the one belonging to the woman who, apologetically, a few minutes later, had asked for a little more gin in her tonic!

Most of the men drank beer, so there was still almost half a bottle of wine left, which Grace shared between their two glasses.

Settling back into her own recliner, she

pointed to the other and said, "Right! Sit comfortably and let the entertainment begin."

Before obeying the command, Seph started removing dirty glasses and squashed beer cans to the kitchen...

Having been run ragged searching for drinks, openers and nibbles on unfamiliar territory, while Grace entertained grandly in the sitting room, she knew where the dishwasher was, and was keen to clear up.

If Mr and Mrs Mather returned to find their immaculate home a wreck, they would never trust her to 'granny-sit' again and, to her own amazement, she was enjoying herself.

"Do sit down, child," Grace kept nagging, "we can do that later. I want to talk to you before Midsomer Murders starts." Seph thought she was about to be asked a string of personal questions, and her heart sank, so she was surprised when Grace asked, "Are you familiar with the series? If not, is there anything about it that you would like to know before it starts?" Seph replied that she had seen a few episodes and enjoyed them, at which Grace nodded happily and switched on the TV.

With the sound muted, as the commercials had not finished, she said, "If there's anything you wish to say, do, ask, or need, can we deal with it now please. Interruptions when it's on will ruin the story for me – I will lose the plot and get upset." Seph had not known Grace very long, but anyone less likely to lose the plot was difficult to imagine; she did understand though, she felt the same when listening to anything.

It was clear that continuing to restore order would be irritating however hard she tried to move stealthily. Being quiet, so obviously, would be even more annoying, so Seph settled down to enjoy the programme. They spoke to each other only during the intervals, when bathroom visits and replenishing drinks and snacks were all accomplished efficiently.

During the two-hour show, Seph noticed that the time was not set on the video recorder so, at the end, she drew attention to the flashing light and offered to set it. Grace surprised her by saying, not to worry, she had unplugged the recorder earlier, to charge something else. She would set it again, herself, before she went to bed, because she wanted to record something on timer during the night.

Seph was amazed. Even her father avoided doing anything with all the electronic gadgetry he bought, other than enjoy it when it was ready to use – it was her mother who pushed buttons and fiddled with switches when things went wrong. Another thumbs-up for Grace!

They cleared away together, before settling down again to watch the news. Contrary to her strict need for silence earlier, Grace commented on almost every item that came up and asked what Seph thought about various world events. Seph found it stimulating. Nobody had taken so much interest in her opinions ever before.

Her knowledge of what was going on around the globe was skimpy, but her interest grew as she paid more attention than she usually did to everything that cropped up, as she watched, from wars, famine and crime to pop stars, fashion and football.

Being able to discuss things straight away was novel.

They didn't agree about everything and sometimes argued at length but, in the end, they were convinced that if they ruled the world it would be a far better place.

When the news finished, Grace clicked from channel to channel before finally switching the set off. "Now what shall we do...?" she asked brightly as if they were just beginning the evening rather than winding down. "Do you like games?"

Before Seph had time to form a cautious answer, not wanting to commit herself to the unknown, they heard son James and his wife, the 'real' Mrs M, returning home.

Grace pushed her recliner button so that she was almost horizontal and winked at Seph, who was not quite sure how to interpret the move, but she soon knew and almost laughed aloud when the rMM entered the room.

"Mother Darling, how are you? We came home as soon as we could get away – we worry about you all the time when we have to leave you..." With a kindly nod towards Seph, she added, "no matter who is looking after you."

"I'm really quite alright, thank you dear," said Grace with a slight quiver in her voice. Thanks to Seph here, I'm still in one piece ...although it was quite frightening at the time."

Their faces were worth watching as Grace described the howling mob on the doorstep and the magnificent way Seph had calmed them all and sorted out the problem.

To avoid being interrogated, Seph decided it was a good time to go. It wasn't easy because Grace was feeding them more and more to whet their curiosity about the problem, while continually praising Seph and saying how clever she'd been.

There was little doubt that she would be invited to sit with Grace again ...or so she thought until she let herself out of the front door. Before it closed, she heard James shout from the kitchen...

"Why in tarnation is the dishwasher full of glasses and the bin full of beer cans? You two must have had one hell of a party!"

Driving home, she sensed Dion in the passenger seat. *"How did it go then, sis?"*

"Why didn't you come in and see for yourself?"

"You know why – but I'm sure it was the best thing to do. It worked, didn't it!"

Relenting, Seph thanked him for supporting her and encouraging her to take over, admitting that he'd helped, and everyone had parted on good terms. He had seen everyone leave and wanted to know why two of the men were singing, arms linked, and why the little woman in the long dress stayed sitting in the middle of the lawn outside, until a car stopped to pick her up. Hugging her holdall and smiling, but with limbs out of control, she'd had to be carried to the car, still crossed-legged.

Dion was eager to hear everything that happened inside, from beginning to end, and even wanted to discuss the plot of Midsomer Murders. Satisfied at last, when Seph said again that he had been brilliant, and she would have gone to pieces without him, he left, smiling broadly, and she drove home alone.

In spite of the fact that she might never be trusted with Grace again, she couldn't help laughing aloud. Unworldly or not, Dion is a typical male. A bit of praise went a long way.

Low, Lower, Lowest

It occurred to Seph, as she took up her daybook again the following day that, if she dwelled completely on the past, current events would have faded by the time she caught up with them, which would be sad. She had enjoyed herself with Grace and didn't want to forget a single moment, so maybe she should write two accounts, past and present, starting with last night.

It wouldn't take her long to change, to go out, and would be several hours until Shell arrived, so she decided to add to her old memories, first. Dion's description of his childhood exploits after her departure would be a good place to start.

He hadn't left the garden for a long time. He felt lost and lonely and bored as time passed.

In earth years he would have been about five years' old before he left the familiarity of the garden. Curiosity eventually overcame him, sitting, waiting, alone in the garden, he'd gradually started to absorb the noises that filled his small world. Identifying the bustling sounds and filtering them to their origin became a game. The 'which bird' game lasted a while – then the 'where is the squirrel', but gradually these fell away next to the questions about 'people noises' as they passed through the garden, weeding, mowing, cleaning, painting and always ignoring him, sitting, patiently on his favourite rock...

Eventually, he became aware of the traffic and people outside the garden and, when the loneliness got too much, he wandered away to investigate.

At first, he was surprised to discover that he was unheard and unseen by the people outside.

Exploring the town, he saw a dog sitting outside a shop and went to pat it. It didn't move or even look at him and he then saw that it wasn't real. Although it was almost as big as he was, he managed to move it and it fell in front of a woman about to enter the shop. She shrieked and he said he was sorry, but of course she couldn't see or hear him!

It amused him for a long time after that, to watch people react when things they put down were not in the same place, when they came back. As he became bolder, he joined a group of people climbing into a bus. It kept stopping and people got on and off. His interest was caught when he saw that there had been an accident on a crossroad... A car coming out had driven into the side of one going in.

Leaving the bus Dion went to hear the two drivers arguing. A child on the back seat of one was crying and instinct made him go inside the car to offer comfort. To his surprise the boy, who was strapped into a seat, could see him and immediately stopped crying. He was too young to converse, but Dion enjoyed playing peek-a-boo with him until his father returned. Dion left them and watched as the car drove away. Eventually he returned to the garden, hoping that I would be back.

Feeling freer now to explore, his confidence grew, so when, one day, he heard voices and laughter not far away, he felt safe enough to go and discover what was happening.

Seeing some children, slightly older than himself, passing the front of our empty house, he followed them and found himself in a school. He enjoyed everything they were doing, especially the games. He found he could deflect the ball when thrown from one to another, or up into a basket. He'd caused chaos for almost two weeks as he haunted the school. Moving books or the teacher's chalk was great fun.

The distant, still living, relative who was supposed to be keeping an eye on him was far too old to cope and Dion took advantage of him. What else could they expect? He was a five-year-old, for goodness sake! Sadly, for him, his grandma found out and he was forbidden to return to earth for years.

It had taken him a long time to build back their confidence, but, finally, the day came when his grandparents agreed that he had become more sensible and proven that he was trustworthy, so he was allowed to come back.

They said he had a lot to learn about the life he'd missed, which would help him to understand those new arrivals who'd had a life and suddenly lost it.

It was a good place to stop, so Seph checked the time and decided to get ready to go out. She could then carry on writing without watching the clock.

Later, settling down at her notebook again she re-read the last few words she had written and took up his story from her sixteenth birthday, after an absence of thirteen years.

He had first shown himself as a child so that I would recognise him, which was clever, because I'd have freaked out, being stalked by an unknown male – perhaps not even aware that he was not of this world.

Dion, to me, looks like a normal living person. He is not wispy or transparent. At first, it was incredibly difficult to accept that he is invisible to others.

"Where have you been – and where do you go when you're not here?" I asked when we met for the first time since childhood. Dion said he went home. "So, you have a home in heaven – what is it like and where is heaven anyway?" I really wanted to know but he didn't seem to understand, so I gave up.

Much later, I discovered that he had no idea what I meant. Never having lived, his knowledge of anything earthly was sadly lacking. I worked out that other spirit people in his world were unlikely to use the description much. We earthly beings talk a lot, but how often do we discuss where we are? Only as we grow up are we told that, if we are good, we go to heaven and, if bad, we go to hell.

I had to accept that my big brother knew less about some things than did the average eight-year-old.

My next question was, "Why do you never come inside the house?" He looked puzzled, shrugged and said Grandma told him never to go anywhere he was not invited, especially if they didn't know he was there. It would be intrusive and very bad form.

"Will I always see you when you are near, or can you hide from me?" was my next query. I must admit I was thinking about bathrooms and bed, so was reassured when he said that whether he was visible to me or not, I would always know when he was with me.

"So, what do you call the place (I almost said where you live – but instantly realised it would be tactless) ...where you are at home?" I persisted. He began to appreciate what I meant and, whilst admitting that he didn't know everything about it, he tried to describe his world.

Apparently, there are higher and lower planes and, when most people die, they leave earth and arrive on the lowest. Because he'd died without being born, and was therefore unsullied, he arrived on a very high one, which, as he opened his eyes and noticed his surroundings, seemed very bright and clear.

His earliest real memories were being cuddled by Grandma, and spending hours helping Granddad in their garden.

As he mixed with other children, he rapidly learned more – not all good – and sank to a lower plane. His curiosity was such that he enjoyed the less saintly company and was happy to explore, but then it wasn't easy to visit his grandparents. They often came down to see him and looked forward to the day when he earned the right to advance again and they could be together more.

They teased him a lot and knew he was not a bad person – 'just like his dad', they told him, so they didn't think it would be difficult for him to learn right from wrong and they advised him, when in doubt, to trust his instincts. Heaven, whether he called it that or not, didn't sound like a fun place, except that he had only to want to be in any other place and he arrived, providing it was on his own or a lower level. Questions like, 'where do you sleep? or, are there buildings you can go into without feeling uncomfortable?' always confused Dion. Earth-speak was hard for him to follow. His previous tasks were all unearthly, like looking after unexpected arrivals 'til their relatives took over and teaching little children how to help each other.

"There seems to be an awful lot of looking after and helping going on. Suppose you don't want to do anything?" I asked. He said that would be unkind and bad people sink lower.

"They might be happier doing what they like lower down," I pointed out, but Dion shook his head. He said they would get bored and be trapped there until they became less selfish.

To me, it sounds like a very boring place altogether and I hope it will be a long time before I find out.

Shell

A glance at the clock told her that Shell would be arriving within twenty minutes, so she tidied her desk. Nobody must come across her scribblings before she was ready to publish!

Why any couple called Fish would decide that Sheila was a good name for their daughter, was beyond Seph ...ever since infant school her friend had been known only as Shell.

The thought side-tracked her ...she wondered what had happened to their other oddly named friends, Rhoda Long and Lucille Pants. Rhoda would only answer to Rhod but, inevitably, Lucille had to put up with Loose.

The four of us had had an hysterical moment at school, suggesting names we might have when we married: if Rhoda became Mrs Hogg would she end up being called Road? Lucille might become Loose Cannon, or Thread or Ends. Lucille said sadly that anything would be better than Pants, and we all agreed, sobering instantly.

Seph and Shell had just joined a book circle and were going to their first meeting tonight. She hoped that widening her reading would help her writing.

Enough for now, Seph decided, refreshing her make-up hastily. Shell would be upset if she had to go into the meeting alone. For a girl who was widely liked and had no problem mixing in a group, she was surprisingly shy about introducing herself to strangers. Mrs Fish blamed herself. She'd reported Shell kidnapped once – frantic when she vanished from her nursery school.

Shell had been told that a neighbour in a green car would pick her up and, when the teacher in charge was looking the other way, Shell happily climbed into the back seat of a green car whose driver left the door open. He had waved and smiled at her as he walked past, so she thought he was there for her.

He returned, carrying a huge pile of

curtaining, which he thrust inside, without looking, before slamming the door shut and driving away. He thought he was alone, until he was ten miles away and, in his rear-view mirror, saw a small head rising slowly from a sea of material.

He braked heavily and the driver of the car that ran into his was no happier than the bus driver, coming from the other direction with a load of hysterical passengers, who had to swerve onto the stony verge. By the time the police arrived and dealt with statements and accusations, there was an all-points bulletin out – a child had been kidnapped.

The experience proved traumatic for Shell and left her confused. Strangers might not be what they seem, but she hadn't known the policemen either and they were kind and had taken her home. Why didn't their kindness outweigh the chaos and shouting strangers?

Seph sympathised, so whenever they met away from home, she always did her best to arrive first. Dion was already in the car when she dropped into the driving seat. *"Are we going somewhere exciting?"* he wanted to know.

"Well, it is a public place, so you could come in, but I doubt whether you'll be interested in books," Seph said. "Although you can read, can't you?"

"Of course I can. I've been to school, but I haven't time to read books. I'm here to learn about living, don't forget. What does 'live it up' mean, by the way?"

Seph was irritated when she realised that he'd gone without waiting for an answer. He was just trying to worry her, so she determinedly put him out of her mind, in order to enjoy the meeting, with Shell.

The Book Circle

Shell was far more excited about the book circle than Seph. Seph liked reading in bed and had books lined up in waiting, so that she was never without one, but Shell carried hers everywhere. In any spare moment, she was eager to catch up on the plot. If she had enjoyed reading one, she wanted her friends to read it too, so that they could talk about it. Seph was afraid that all the members of the circle would be the same but was prepared to cooperate to keep Shell happy.

The meeting was in the back room of a pub, so there was bar service. The second rule, they learned as they booked in, was that refreshments for the interval must be pre-ordered and paid for, although drinks could be bought and taken into the meeting at the start.

The first rule was no surprise – even before going in, mobile phones must be switched off.

The secretary informed them primly that social pleasantries beforehand were an important part of members' enjoyment, creating a mood, removing them from every-day cares. "That's what we all do when we open a book, isn't it," she added rhetorically, "we step into another world and forget our own for a while."

True to character as always, Shell nudged Seph when she saw two middle-aged men closing in on them rapidly in a pincer movement. "I'll get the drinks," she said, backing into the lobby that led to the bar. She would relax once she'd met them in a group, but one to one, she would be tongue-tied.

One man was clutching two name-badges, which were to be clipped on to any convenient part of their clothing he advised, with no hint of crudity, although he scarcely lifted his eyes above her chest level as he handed them over. This might have been because he was at least six inches shorter, so she gave him the benefit of the doubt and continued to smile.

The other gave her several sheets of paper for them to share, relating to the meeting, and two identical stapled sets, which he hoped they would find time to read before the second half. Checking the agenda, her heart sank. Someone was writing her autobiography and wanted feedback on her first chapter... Incredible – everyone was at it! She wondered what they would think if they ever read hers.

Everyone was taking seats and coming to order at the end of the room so the two men, Edward and George according to their badges, were obviously in a hurry. They kept interrupting each other like a double act, moving her steadily with them, hoping her friend would not be long, leading her to their allotted places. Apparently, the chairman liked everyone to be seated and quiet before he joined them!

It was an impressive use of the room's space. Fifteen small card tables were arranged to form a gentle curve, just wide enough for two people to share a table and still get a clear view of the proceedings. Three more tables were set in a straight line, in the centre. These were littered with piles of folders, in the middle of which stood a microphone on a stand. That must be for the committee, Seph guessed and, to her discomfort, she and Shell were placed directly opposite it.

She hoped Shell would return soon with stiff drinks – she had a feeling that they were going to need them! Before she sat, she was introduced to two women who were already seated: the wife of George the badge-bearer and, the other, a stunning blonde who was married to Edward, although less than half his age. They were all sitting together but, as Edward was still animatedly putting her in the picture about what to expect, Seph sat next to him leaving Shell to cope with George and Mildred.

Did all Georges marry Mildreds? The idle thought distracted her for a moment and she missed hearing the blonde's name. She also lost the gist of Edward's apology and thought he had done something specifically unforgivable but soon realised that he was worried about the manuscript pages that everyone had to read.

"We always hand over the second half of the meeting to any volunteer member who wishes to talk about something specifically connected to our love of books." He sighed and shook his head, obviously embarrassed. "We have never before encouraged anyone to present their unpublished work for criticism."

As far as Seph could gather, the hopeful authoress was a founder member of the circle and nobody wanted to upset her by turning down her offer to read the extract and discuss her own life story.

There was barely time to relay all this to Shell before the meeting started, but they both scrutinised their three pages during the opening formalities.

Members had received advance copies and were following the Chairman's words keenly. When everyone looked at the two visiting guests and clapped in welcome, both George and Edward hastened to call their attention back to matters in hand. When nothing happened after the clapping died down, Edward whispered to Seph, "Just say a few words to introduce yourselves – you first."

Seph spoke briefly and finished by saying she was looking forward to the meeting. Shell ignored the fact that her badge clearly said 'Shell'.

Giving her name as Sheila Fish, she told them that she worked in the Customer Services department of a local electronic store. Reading was her passion, but she had no urge to be a writer. She started to say that, even if she did, she would never write an autobiography because why would anyone be interested in it unless she became a celebrity, which of course she never would...

When Seph grabbed her skirt, she immediately sat down looking somewhat bemused. Fortunately, Seph told her later, everything she said after 'autobiography' was probably lost to all who were not sitting close to them.

The first half of the evening, an open discussion based on romantic novels, was organised chaos but actually good fun. A very sprightly woman darted about with the mike and thrust it under speakers' noses, always dashing away before they had quite finished. Those with good hearing may well have heard every word and deaf people were used to guessing what was said anyway so Seph supposed it probably didn't matter.

During the interval, which was greeted, by all, with enthusiasm (especially the mike carrier and those who had ordered drinks) the two girls were made to feel welcome by everyone they met. Several hoped they would decide to join – it would be such a benefit to the circle to have input from young, intelligent people.

Shell was cornered by the member who was about to conduct the second half of the evening. Fortunately, a bell suddenly trilled and, as if remotely controlled, everyone turned and moved back to their seats. Seph could see that Shell was upset but could only guess why, until the woman started to speak.

Her first words made Seph squirm... "Perhaps it was unwise of me to show it to anyone before it was thoroughly edited but I am so excited to have started writing. I have actually had an unusually interesting life so far," she added, looking directly at Shell.

Later, on the way home, Shell defended herself. "The woman shouldn't invite criticism if she can't stand the truth... I only said it to her anyway; not to the whole gathering. Rotten grammar and four typos in the first paragraph and so many errors following that I couldn't concentrate on the plot: if there was one!"

"Never mind," Seph tried to console her. "You will undoubtedly get a chance to read it again when she's had it checked over and then you can bite your tongue. Let's face it, she's hardly likely to get it finished, let alone published, she must be ninety if she's a day."

As the meeting room emptied, Letitia Ledbetter, in spite of her eighty-three years, was helping to put the tables back in place for the bridge club meeting tomorrow morning. She was bubbling with excitement, not only because she felt her reading had gone well – people looked forward to hearing more of her thrilling life, but she'd found the answer to all her prayers.

"That young Shelley spoke to me during the break and said I really needed help with the grammar and to pick up all my silly little typing errors. I'm not getting any younger and have been worried that I've left it too late to start, but now, I am so happy. Please email me her contact details, she forgot to give them to me. She's a lovely girl – we will make a perfect team..."

Another member requested telephone numbers for both girls, but it was Seph, in particular, that Margot wanted to get to know.

Saturday, all day

The morning after the book circle meeting was unusually busy. Saturdays were normally days of late rising, as were Sundays too for Seph; she rarely went to church. Her parents were unpredictable, so unless they specifically told her they would be going to morning service, to make her feel guilty, she enjoyed lying in bed reading. They accepted that she might not wish to go to worship regularly but felt duty-bound, occasionally, to remind her that professions of faith needed renewing.

Seph, after exchanges with Dion, was no longer sure what to believe. The Heaven he described, although not calling it that, was nothing like her imagination had pictured;

she'd seen it as a floating, cloudy place where winged angels sang and a bearded man with a glittering crown and long, curly hair, sat smiling on a huge throne.

It now sounded to her a lot like Earth, but without weighty law enforcement. The controlling body, headed by an all-seeing boss, must consist of mind-readers: no need for courts, judges and juries. Everyone understood that whether they moved higher or lower depended on their own behaviour. Their ultimate fate was in their own hands.

Although now on a lower plane, Dion had glimpsed, briefly, a beautiful, bright place where, he was sure, all souls wanted to end up. So, when people said that Hell was another name for Earth, perhaps they were right. Dion was no help; he had never heard of Hell either!

Such silly thoughts flitted through Seph's head as she left the house and drove away. She had let herself out quietly as it was only eight-o-clock.

Once a month, Seph looked after 'Maggie's Mags', the local newspaper shop that sold more sweets than papers.

Maggie had to attend regular monthly appointments at the hospital to have blood tests, to indicate the correct daily dosage of one of her pills for the following month. As long as she obeyed the instructions on the chart, taking anything from a quarter to a whole tablet every morning, there was nothing to worry about – she was 'as fit as a fiddle' she claimed.

An ambulance picked up Maggie at half-past-eight and delivered her back home three hours later, and she really looked forward to her morning off.

The queue for the tests was long and she might have anything up to an hour to wait for her turn, but all the regulars were like old friends, and exchanged gossip eagerly as if at a party. The ambulance trip took almost an hour each way, because it trundled in and out of villages for miles around, transporting patients; Maggie said she could be there and back on her bike in a quarter of the time, but she enjoyed being driven in style.

Fortunately, Seph enjoyed her duties at the shop.

On arrival, Maggie always briefed her

carefully, providing written lists of reserved copies of newspapers and magazines, over and above regular orders, so that only spare ones would be on the counter. There was nothing else to it really... keeping an eye on kids near the sweets was likely to be the worst part.

She could look forward to leafing through a few glossies ...not new ones of course; Maggie always kept a few out-of-date copies under the counter. They were destined for the hospital, but it was great having something on hand to read. Dion would also be on hand! He didn't mind going into shops without an invitation because anyone could.

It was quite reassuring knowing he was there, keeping an eye on the long racks that ran the length of the shop. She didn't always see him but, on one occasion, a toddler was trying to play with Dion and having temper tantrums when his mother kept dragging him away. The poor woman could not know that his hysterical giggles were due to the funny faces Dion was making.

There was only one other customer who, she was sure, could see her ghostly brother. The young man in question, whose eyes were constantly darting sideways at Dion while waiting to be served, never queried his presence, but didn't seem to accept him as just another customer until Dion, one day, picked up a book and opened it. Whilst the man left seemingly reassured that Dion was a customer and not a thief 'casing the joint', to Seph's amusement, she realised that a third person was watching, who couldn't see Dion.

Luckily, it was an unpleasant child who loved pinching her baby brother whenever their mother wasn't looking. Just as she was poised to pinch, she saw the book floating, hovering, and returning to the rack, and was scared stiff. After that, at least in the shop, her behaviour changed... never sure whether or not unseen eyes were on her, she wouldn't leave her mother's side.

It was not often that Seph's duty mornings fell on a Saturday and she was glad not to have to cope with school kids on their way to and from school. They all wanted to be served first, hardly ever gave the right money and screeched non-stop.

At the weekends, most customers were adults who seldom lingered, apart from the older ones enjoying a chat, blocking the aisles. It was funny though, watching them moving away together, as one, whenever an '*excuse me please*' managed to make itself heard above their lively conversation. Eventually, their stately, grand tour of the entire shop would bring them to the counter and their purchases were always a weird assortment.

Anything that caught their eye while standing still, went into their baskets. Pencil sharpeners, crayons, rubber bands, wrapping paper, road maps, envelopes, greeting cards: such a variety that Seph couldn't help wondering which item, if any, was the one that had brought them into the shop.

It was impossible not to eavesdrop.

Today, the oldest of three women, whose daughter was in the middle of a divorce, eagerly launched into all the latest developments – it was gripping stuff and Seph began to despise the adulterous swine of a husband as much as his mother-in-law did.

"Never you mind, Martha, if he tries to cheat

her of her rights, he'll be the one to suffer in the end, you mark my words," comforted one of the others who felt well qualified to pass judgement, as she had worked in an advice bureau for a few years. Turning to the other member of the group she asked, "Did your grandson get the job he was after?"

The short round person addressed was clearly not comfortable, having to say that her grandson was still unemployed. "He's a lovely lad," she added, "I know he is untrained but he's ever so willing to turn his hand to anything. We all told him, years ago that he shouldn't keep playing truant, but he was frightened of going to school – the girls wouldn't leave him alone – chasing him all the time, they were. He missed his exams, so has no qualifications on paper, but that shouldn't matter, should it?"

"Didn't Maggie offer him a job a few months ago?" Martha asked, exchanging a knowing look with their friend.

"But being a paper-delivery boy at twenty-three-years-old is hardly much of a job and he'd have had to get up at five every morning ...not what he's looking for at all. Freddy is really keen to do something that will make his parents proud of him."

The fond grandma heard Seph's derisory laugh and turned to frown at her.

Pointing to the magazine she held, Seph indicated how funny it was, by smiling widely.

It had suddenly dawned on Seph that she knew the grandson. Way back, before she went to Uni, they were at the same school. Far from being pursued by girls, most of them were indifferent and the others positively disliked him. They'd hardly seen him at school at all during the final year and if rumours ever reached them, about freaky Fred's excuses for sneaking off school, they would be hysterical – what a nerve! So, he was still around; she hoped she wouldn't run into him, it didn't sound as if he'd changed: still a loser.

The three women, happily chatting, shifting and shuffling to make way for passing traffic, were whispering now and glancing in her direction, making Seph feel uncomfortable. She wished she knew what they were saying.

Dion was at the far end of the shop but suddenly, as if close to her ear, she heard him say, *"They think you're gorgeous and wonder why you aren't married. You must be over twenty, so you are probably sleeping with someone, that's what girls do these days, but they are going to find out, because Freddy hasn't got a steady girlfriend and you are just what he needs."*

Dion paused, as if for breath (she really must stop analysing the differences between the living and the dead) ...then he asked, *"What do they mean? I don't like the sound of it!"*

"Neither do I," she muttered, "but thanks for the warning."

Seph was not surprised when, at the counter on their way out, they tried to 'draw her out'... They remembered her name, had not seen her in the shop for a long while, although she lived in the village, so perhaps she had another job during the week ...and so on, and on. It was fortunate that the queue was growing rapidly so they had to move out.

The last person to reach the till was a woman whose face was familiar – she had met her fleetingly somewhere. In a flash, Seph remembered and greeted her, "Oh, hello, we met at the book club, didn't we?"

"Circle dear, we call ourselves a circle. I can only think it's to stop people confusing us with a lending library." She smiled kindly, obviously not meaning her correction to sound like a rebuke. "I'm pleased to see you again because I understand that you are free during the next few months to take on little jobs: so much more satisfying than wasting time."

Seph was somewhat taken aback, but eager to hear what the job required was and said she was willing to tackle anything within reason – not adding 'legal', which might have implied that she thought it could be anything other!

"I'm quite confident that you would find the job palatable," said her customer, "and, to be honest, if you turn it down it will stay undone." The woman was patently pleased at the mixed expression of puzzlement and interest that crossed Seph's face and held out her hand to shake. "I'm Margot, by the way, Margot Grant. I hope we can do business together."

Someone, frantically waving money, was likely to be upset if Seph ignored him, so she scribbled Margot's telephone number on the desk calendar and promised to ring soon. Putting the Birthday Card in a paper bag with his loose change, Seph noted that it said 'Belated' ...

"I hope you catch the post," she couldn't resist calling to the man's back as he hurtled towards the door. His sickly grin as he cast a stricken glance over his shoulder made her wish she had not been facetious... Would she never learn!

Early Evening

In the car on the way home, Seph questioned Dion about the nature of the job that was being offered to her – surely, he must have an inkling. He was too preoccupied to answer immediately. He liked sitting properly in the passenger seat and insisted on strapping himself in, so Seph kept a travel blanket handy to throw over the waving belts. Casual observers would think nothing of a covered object, and she found it less distracting.

"How should I know," Dion replied, still playing with the buckle, *"I'm more interested in what they said about you – those grandmas in the shop."*

"Being old doesn't necessarily mean that they are grandmas," Seph retorted impatiently. What do you mean anyway? You were the one who heard them."

"Yes, but are they right – should you really be married? And who is the somebody you must be sleeping with? And what is the point of being with another person anyway, if you are asleep?"

Seph sighed heavily – it was going to be another long teaching session. She reminded herself that learning about life was the reason for his being back on earth. When his Guardian told him that he must learn about life in order to make progress, he had leaped at the chance to nominate his sister as his tutor in chief.

Seph, intrigued when he first spoke of guardians, discovered that it was what teachers were called on the other side and Dion went on to say that the place where they taught was Excelsior. He was puzzled when Seph asked if it was the name of the school. Dion supposed so; he said the word 'Excelsior' shimmered above all the guardians, so it must be the name of their school. *"Mustn't it?"* he added, as if talking to a real thickie. *"And they all stay together in their school... Like fish,"* he added with a grin.

Seph knew that Excelsior meant something

like 'Onward and Upwards' so it was probably a good name for a school. The guardian who sent him earthbound was Number One – Godfrey – the boss; Granddad's best friend, Dion claimed proudly, and he was determined not to let him down.

When she commented on how lucky he was that, apparently, everyone in heaven spoke English, Dion laughed. He knew people from all over the world and however they spoke, he heard them in his own language – just as they understood him in theirs. Seph thought she'd sound him out and said, "Ou est ma Chat?"

"Don't be silly," he replied, *"You haven't got a cat!"*

In the last four years, they had learned a lot from each other – but it still took Seph by surprise when, in many ways, he was extraordinarily innocent. Now, it was evident that when it came to sex, love and marriage, he knew far less than the average child.

By the time they arrived home, Dion was quite clear about the difference between sleeping and 'sleeping with' and, just for good measure, Seph threw in 'sleeping around'.

She made it clear that such behaviour was foolhardy, indulged in only by those who lacked self-worth and self-restraint. The lesson ended there when she went into the house.

The questions Dion had asked during her explanation were ingenuous and often personal. If he had always been there, growing up with her, older and wiser, she could imagine how he would have kept a watchful eye on her and assessed any new boyfriends she might have. She wondered how watchful his eyes had been over the years, but quickly shrugged off such thoughts – she was no angel, but certainly had nothing to be ashamed of!

She would like to have recorded the day's events in her book, while fresh in her mind, but she was anxious to ring Margot Grant. What kind of job could it possibly be, if only she was considered eligible to undertake it? Seph had never been unduly modest but even to herself she was no superwoman.

Twenty minutes later, although still no wiser about her unique attributes, she at least had an idea what Margot wanted, and was going to Sunday tea, to talk about it.

When she went down to dinner later, she told her mother about the appointment.

Her mother always looked forward to chatting to Seph about how her jobs were working out and her curiosity was piqued too, by the mystery surrounding the promised job.

"I knew George Grant before they married, although we were never close friends and I've never met his wife – but her mother was, probably still is, a writer," she informed Seph. "It might stand you in good stead if you looked her up before you visit. Her name is Victoria Millais, but I have a feeling she wrote under a nom de plume."

Much of Seph's afternoon was devoted to research, but finally she discovered that under the name Tricia Millais, Victoria had written three non-fiction books on travel in the Far East, all now out of print. It was possible that Margot's family had travelled a lot, or perhaps lived abroad when she was young.

To be on the safe side, although not able to find the books, Seph enjoyed surfing through expatriate life in the mid-20th century. It might not have been much fun to be caught up in jungle warfare or skirmishes in the South China Sea, but it sounded anything but dull. Even in black and white pictures at embassy receptions, the young women positively glowed on the arms of their incredibly handsome escorts.

Intermittently, her mind went back to the Freaky Freddy supporters' club and their speculation about her love life. He had pestered her for a while but Seph had always regarded attention from males as normal... They merely wanted to make a conquest, before going on to the next female and she wouldn't play that game! Only in her late-teens did she notice that her refusal to go 'all the way' seemed to increase her popularity and often upset other girls. Some of them would go to any length to acquire a boyfriend and it did them no good at all. The feckless males moved on to other easy meat. She didn't mind being labelled prudish, she was just not attracted to men who followed this pattern.

She felt sorry for the girls they left behind, in their self-centred trail, and wanted nothing to do with any man who could be so heartless.

It was probably unrealistic, in the current sexual climate, to expect her future husband also to be a virgin, but there was no harm in hoping.

She was lucky that Shell and her other close friends were of the same mind and they shared a great social life. The men in their lives were used to dating mostly in foursomes and, over the years, although some couples had married, all remained friends.

They had a date tonight, but Seph had forgotten where and decided to text Shell before adding a page or two to her book ... *whr r we mtg 2nite n w@ tym?* Almost immediately Shell replied, *Idk whr but my car b@ry died so cn u pik me ^ @ 7pm plz? Ill fnd out whr Joe's prt s. itz hs bday. cul8r.*

Good – she had plenty of time to add more of her recollections about Dion's description of 'heaven'.

She tried to picture him looking after new arrivals and could understand how the sudden transition from earth might cause a lost soul a certain measure of panic...

I asked if he looked after children only, and Dion said that new arrivals were happy to be met by anyone, young or old, when their passing had been unexpected.

Everybody has relatives who once lived on earth, who are eager to meet them again; if they die on schedule there's no problem, but sudden death causes panic on both sides of the veil.

I was curious to know if all babies eventually return to earth, but Dion thought most of them did not. They grow up happily with their families and have no curiosity about lower levels.

Before she had time to start writing again, the house phone rang, and, moments later, her mother shouted from the bottom of the stairs... "Pick up quickly please. You are wanted by the police!"

The urgency in the tone of voice would have been enough to make Seph grab her passport and dash to the nearest airport, had she been of guilty even of littering. Luckily, having a clear conscience, she had no qualms, only curiosity, and lifted the receiver off the cradle and announced herself.

"Persephone Montague speaking... May I help you?"

"DC Pickering here: I believe you were looking after Maggie's this morning?"

When Seph confirmed that the statement was correct, he said that her presence at the local police station was required urgently. "You might have witnessed something of importance. There was a serious incident at a property opposite the shop and we have photographs we'd like you to look at." He added that if she needed transport a car could be dispatched to pick her up. On being assured that she would prefer to drive herself, the Detective Constable said they would expect her in ten minutes.

The implication was that, if she were not there in ten minutes, she would be prosecuted for something and found guilty. Seph was extremely annoyed, but curious.

She grabbed her bag and ran.

Shouting goodbye to anyone within hearing, she left the house, so the gist of her mother's shouted reply did not hit her until she flung herself into the driving seat ...Murder! ...Someone had been murdered. Dion was in the passenger seat, already belted up and ready to go – shaking with excitement. *"Hurry up, we're witnesses,"* he said.

He had mentioned before that, had he lived, he would have been a greater detective than Sherlock Holmes and, when reminded that Holmes was a character in a book, refused to back down. *"We'll be shown mug-shots and I'll know straight away which one is guilty. I am very observationalist,"* he reminded her again now."

"You mean 'observant'," she corrected him as they drove off. "You've been to America again, haven't you?"

"Yes, I think so. I went to the bull fights," he grinned.

"You must have been in Spain then. Really, your geography is worse than mine. I would have thought you could see the world laid out like a map."

"Don't be silly – even if I was up in the sky on a cloud, countries wouldn't have names on them, would they?"

Seph had to admit he had a valid point and, anyway, they were turning into the police station car park and there was no time to argue. She had scarcely looked out of the shop window herself, so had very little hope of being able to help. Only as she locked the car, did she suddenly start worrying about how much Dion had really seen. It might be better to say she had seen nothing rather than misdirect their investigation.

Murder was a serious subject and he would treat it like a game – a game into which she could not avoid being drawn, unless she kept her wits about her. He was still sitting inside and, clearly aware of her misgivings, gave her a very slow wink before fading away.

Meanwhile...

All members of the Grant household were enjoying Saturday at home, but not together. The teenage girls, Zoey and Zena were in their rooms playing computer games and texting each other. Father was gardening, and Margot was watching a DVD with Daniel, their youngest son, in the sitting room. They had similar taste in films and he always made sure that they had a choice of several to tide them over the weekend.

Her husband, George, would go to the study when he'd finished his chores – he was much happier computing and running his web-building business than doing what other people referred to as relaxing.

Daniel knew dozens of people who would have welcomed his company, but he only ever left home when it was unavoidable and, even then, seemed sorry to have to go out.

He had always been happy with his own company and started writing short stories, which were published, when he was a barely in his teens.

At twenty-five, he was an established author, with a degree in psychology, if ever he needed to work more conventionally. After all, as he liked to point out, Katharine Hepburn, Playboy's Hugh Hefner and Ted Bundy the serial killer all read psychology at university and were never employed on the strength of it! The only one of the three he might follow was Hefner but, if he did, his magazine would certainly not be voyeuristic.

Margot loved his books – as did the reading public thank goodness, she thought – but most of his readers never suspected that his written opinions of women were close to his own. If they did, they seemed to regard it as a challenge, wanting to be the one who made him see that not all girls were money-grabbing opportunists.

She regretted having expected his older brothers to look after him so often, when he was younger. They were only five and six years older but responsible enough to care for him. Unfortunately, the girls they entertained were not above flirting and teasing a child. Only later did Margot learn that to protect him, the brothers had thought that sending him to bed with a games machine was a good idea. Thank goodness they had eventually married young women she could like.

Daniel was highly intelligent and observant. Being a keen reader of newspapers and magazines as well as books, he was very much aware of their influence and the effect they might have on everyone who read them.

Of course, although his siblings' adolescent girlfriends had provided material for his novels, it had also soured him, damaging his personal relationships, and Margot blamed herself. For years she had tried to overcome his cynicism... Her current plan had to succeed, and it all rested on the young woman she would be interviewing tomorrow.

At the Station

Within minutes of announcing herself at the desk, Seph was taken to a room at the back of the police station that looked very like a cell, where two men, obviously senior detectives, were already seated. They introduced themselves, indicating with pleasant smiles that she should join them.

They informed her that a serious crime had been committed at around eleven-thirty that morning; they wanted her to tell them everything she could remember about anything she had seen from the shop window.

Now that she was involved in the investigation, Seph was excited by the implication that she could help and reluctant to disappoint them by saying she'd had enough to look after, inside the shop, and hadn't glanced outside at all.

Among an array of photographs on the

notice board was one of a house that she recognised: it must be the one where someone was murdered. She shuddered.

Not having anything to report herself, Seph needed Dion and was relieved that he had joined her.

She was aware that Dion was studying the pictures and not surprised when he gave her a thumbs-up and a delighted grin. It was inappropriate that he should be smiling happily but, if he helped her to help the police, she would forgive him.

She spoke and let Dion's words flow out as she heard them, without too much thought... "I think it was about half-past-ten when I saw someone at the front door, and an elderly man let him in." This caused a flurry of excitement and more questions.

"Was it a man you recognised?"

"How was the man dressed?"

"Would you recognise him again?"

When her answers – 'no', 'track suit' and 'probably' – had been taken on board, she was offered a cup of tea to drink and sheaves of photos to look through.

"Mug-shots!" Dion yelled in her ear and Seph threw a startled look around – amazed that nobody else had heard him. *"I told you so. Turn the pages... Hurry."*

As she sipped her tea and flipped through dozens of pictures, she sensed disappointment growing in the two detectives. One could not resist pointing to a few and asking her if she was sure they were not the caller who entered the house. Seph had enough faith in Dion to say she was sure, because she knew he was as disappointed as she was herself that the murderer was not among the suspects.

The man who was obviously the more senior of the two said, "If we'd found fingerprints at the scene we could have checked this lot, but an identification would have given us a good reason to bring them in for questioning. There's always a chance that one will shop another if they're scared."

"But you *can* get his DNA," Seph found herself saying confidently. It was just as well that the men were stupefied and said nothing for a moment; it allowed her to recover too. She only hoped Dion was not making up all this, but had to trust him, having committed herself.

"I don't know what time it was when he came out, but when he walked down the steps from the door, he was just finishing drinking something. He threw the empty can into the bin at the gate." Seph had never seen anyone move as fast. Boss-man pointed to the door and number two shot out.

She was thanked effusively, and her hand was shaken heartily as she was ushered out and told to expect a call from them soon. Within a few minutes, she was back in the car park watching a police car speeding out in the direction of Maggie's Mags. Dion shrugged, *"I don't know why they're breaking the speed limit – surely they know that refuse and recycling collection officers are off the job now until Monday."*

Seph boggled quietly – Dion could be amazingly pompous sometimes. *"No, I am not!"* He said, in his hurt, misunderstood voice, making Seph feel like a worm.

"I am really impressed," she said, "that you know so much about bin-men and speed limits ...that sort of stuff. Your earthly education is coming on well. Do you have to sit exams?" Dion immediately cheered up and shook his head, so Seph changed the subject. "I'm going to a birthday party tonight – what are you doing?"

"I'm going to watch 'Heaven Can Wait'; it's a comedy about a man trying to get into Hell."

"Where is it on – surely not locally – anyway it's about a man who goes to heaven by mistake and can't get back because his body has been cremated."

"No, it isn't. I know the plot," Dion insisted, *"I've seen it twice already because I like Marjorie Main – she's a friend of Grandma's."* He shot her a triumphant glance and Seph knew he had tricked her deliberately, same title – years earlier ...so she repeated her query about where it was showing.

She was no wiser when he said it was on a big screen on a hill, but from his description of the audience, it sounded as if it must be at an army camp on the other side of the world. She must try to improve his knowledge of the planet. It would be good for her too.

At least he would not be hanging about with her at Joe's. She could relax and enjoy herself –

if she got a move on; Shell was expecting her in less than an hour.

From Caversham Heights, where she lived, to Shell's home in the town centre, would take about fifteen minutes.

After crossing the river, the traffic was heavier, but it thinned out on the other side of Reading, where the party was.

Seph was good at getting ready in haste. She'd had plenty of practise. She always became totally absorbed in whatever she was doing, prior to going out, losing track of time. Her success at speedy exits was due, in part, to her good fortune in having naturally wavy hair that fell into place with one combing when wet, then dried smoothly to flatter her heart-shaped face.

She didn't own masses of clothes but always hung them by type and having decided on a colour could select a suitable outfit in seconds. Her record from entering the bathroom to dashing out of the front door, according to her father, was twelve minutes forty-five seconds. She wore so little makeup that she applied what she needed during traffic-light stops.

Racing into the house, she was waylaid by her mother, who was understandably anxious to hear what had happened, so, of course, Seph had to stop, mid-flight, to tell her. She felt slightly guilty taking the credit for the possible clue, but she could not bring Dion into it – his presence would take a lot more than a few minutes to explain!

"I'm amazed that you saw anything at all," exclaimed Jill. "Your father and I have always lamented that you are the most unobservant person on earth. Isn't that so Jack?" Seph's father looked up briefly from his newspaper and agreed.

As she hurriedly excused herself and hastened away, Seph couldn't help laughing as her mother's words floated after her... "You really are the limit Jack, you haven't heard a word your daughter said! You are worse than she is ...but perhaps we've been wrong. Now just listen..."

Party Night

Despite the delay, Seph picked up Shell five minutes earlier than arranged and they had no traffic problem reaching Joe's flat. He and his partner Jeremy lived on the third floor of a modern block and, although the neighbours were on the young side of middle-aged, nobody appreciates hearing other people carousing into the early hours, so, before midnight, the party moved on to a local night club.

Not all in the party stayed the course, but about ten went with their hosts to carry on celebrating. The club was a favourite although none of the girls would have ventured there alone; it was surrounded by sleazy bars and unsavoury drunks, who clung to anything, or anyone, within reach.

The partygoers spilled out of Jeremy's People Carrier leaving him to drive off and park elsewhere. They didn't wait for him, parking was almost impossible; he had once ended up so far away that he had taken a taxi back.

Shell turned at the entrance and saw Seph still at the kerb. "Come on – what are you staring at? Seen a ghost?" In fact, Seph had. Dion had emerged from the car with her.

"What are you doing here," she asked him mentally, "I thought you were watching a film."

"The tape broke – it happens a lot out there, so I'm having a night on the tiles instead."

"Do you know what that means? Never mind – just don't startle anyone. Appearing and disappearing might be fun for you, but it isn't for some. Fortunately, most people are not psychic, but please take care."

"Yes sis, your wish is my command ...anyway it wasn't my fault when that guy drove into a lamp post – he was drunk anyway. I probably saved him from driving into bigger trouble!" With a mock salute, he disappeared and Seph realised that Shell was calling to her.

Over the next two hours, Dion floated in and out several times and Seph began to think he was keeping an eye on her alcohol consumption, but he said the place was dull in comparison to the others on the street and didn't stay. The party was about to break up and Jeremy, fortunately a non-drinker, had gone for his car, to transport them back to theirs. when Dion suddenly appeared again, extremely agitated and pleading with her to go with him... and to call the police. *"I've seen him – he's across the road – bring muscles!"*

Seph knew immediately that he must have spotted the person who threw his empty can in the bin. She must think of an excuse to go to the other bar – and, in about ten minutes, the car would come to pick them up. Hurrying everyone outside, so at least the bar was in sight, Seph rapidly threw caution to the winds and shouted to get everyone's attention.

They all knew of the murder and her involvement as a witness, so when she pointed and said she thought the wanted man had just gone through that door, but needed to make sure, they were keen to help. The plan was improvised quickly. Seph would go inside the bar escorted by three of the men. The others would stay outside, but one would get the police on the phone and keep the operator busy until they had a thumbs-up signal.

They couldn't risk losing sight of him and the suspect getting away but didn't want to get into a fight either.

When Seph saw Dion inside, she was reassured. He was not smiling – his look was determined and confident.

He beckoned and walked to the far end of the room but told her to stop when she was halfway through the throng. On her right, sitting on a stool, was the person he wanted her to identify. She couldn't see the man's face! Staring into the mirror beyond him, which reflected the top of his head, was of little help.

She couldn't hover behind him much longer; what could she do? Dion, of course, came to her rescue. For no reason that anyone else could see, a full mug of beer suddenly tipped over and the cold liquid poured into the lap of the man Seph needed to identify.

When he yelled and fell backwards at her feet, his face was close and, distinguishable by lip and brow studs, was quite unforgettable, should he get away again.

Within minutes of her nod to Joe, who was waiting at the entrance, and his signal to the rest of the gang outside, two uniformed police officers arrived with a van.

Seph and her friends were sensible enough to wait outside to tell them that the man they wanted was at the bar and to describe him and his clothing.

After making a call to the station and satisfying themselves that Seph was a legitimate witness and likely to be right, they went in and arrested him.

So, the party ended spectacularly and, as a result of Seph's intervention, the police solved their murder case in an impressive sixteen hours. Of course, this wouldn't become public knowledge for several months but when it did, Seph wondered, could she add 'Private Investigator' to her list of services? *"Come off it, big head, you'd have been nowhere without me,"* Dion butted into her thoughts.

Her sudden burst of laughter did not give rise to comment – her companions were all buoyed by her success. They laughed with her, all the way home.

Sunday

Unlike every other day of the week, the Grant family always made an effort to have Sunday lunch together at home, or at least to enjoy pre-lunch drinks. Even the older boys and their wives turned up to eat, more often than not. After all, it was only half of the day and all their favourite shops would be shut. They always knew what the meal would be; not roast beef, but curry, Indonesian style, which Margot regarded as traditional because her mother had always cooked it on Sundays.

Margot's mother, now in her eighties still drove herself round every week to help with all the sambals and poppadums that traditionally accompanied the meal. She always stayed until early evening but, today, would remain out of sight in the study watching TV, while Margot entertained Seph for tea. She hoped to meet Seph, if all went well, because the germ of the idea had come from her.

Victoria was sixteen when her family moved to Singapore. Her father, a Colonel in the British Army had decided that three years in the Far East would be a more beneficial experience for her than time spent at boarding school. Her mother was delighted because, otherwise, she would have refused to join him. He had not been aware that she felt so strongly about being parted from her only child by so many thousands of miles.

As it transpired, he might not have taken his family with him had he known that a war was brewing.

The communists in Malaya were a big problem but when serious guerrilla warfare broke out between them and the Commonwealth armed forces in 1948, it was described as an Emergency. Rubber plantation owners and tin mining industries' losses would not have been covered by insurance policies, had it been called a war!

It didn't end until 1960, long after the family returned to England, but her three years as an army brat in a foreign station made a lasting impression on Victoria and stood her in good stead. Father was right!

The problem of safeguarding a young daughter, in the midst of possible chaos, was pressing. Not willing to leave her alone with only an Amah when they went out at night, the solution was to take Victoria with them. Her father was, more often than not, on duty on such outings and it was difficult to keep an eye on her, without embarrassing her.

The biggest headache was the fact that she was not only one of very few English girls living anywhere near the army camp, she was not short of admirers. Colonel Millais' solution was to vet every officer under his command thoroughly.

Those with reputations for drinking and partying, or familiarity with local girls did not even make his short list. Some were not suitable because they were unattached, but one was a man he really liked; it was therefore Captain Martin Montague who was invited to be Victoria's official and willing escort, whenever she needed one.

Being allowed to attend everything, from

Mess dinners and Balls to the frequent tea and garden parties thrown by the married officers' wives, was thrilling for Victoria. Some of the best buffet parties she had ever attended were in the Messes ...and she went to every event on the arm of Martin Montague.

He was tall and handsome, and she adored him. The fact that he carried everywhere with him a wallet full of photographs of his fiancée and spoke about his wedding plans at every opportunity made it easy for Victoria to relax.

With most young men, she had to watch every word she spoke in case they thought she was flirting or encouraging them. He was six years older and planning to marry his Pamela in 1952.

Many years later, on a whim, she had traced him, through his army career and eventual retirement. Amazingly, his home was only a few miles away. Her husband was as pleased as she was, and they both agreed to contact him; a foursome for dinner would be wonderful and she would meet Pamela – they were sure to become friends.

Unfortunately, both Martin and Pamela had

died. She was a year too late. She started keeping an eye on their son Jack and his family, almost feeling that, in a funny sort of way, she was repaying Martin for watching over her.

She was not surprised when the Montagues' daughter was christened Persephone.

Martin had never tired of talking about Greek Myths and legends and they had once worked through dozens of Greek Gods and Goddesses, whose names would shorten to fit in with the modern world. The first two on the list were Persephone and Dionysus. Pamela had clearly NOT shared his obsession as their son was named Jacob.

Ironically, he must not only have disliked his biblical name shortening it to Jack, he appeared to share his father's fascination with Greek Gods and had obviously influenced his own wife, when it came to naming their daughter – good for him!

It was a pity they didn't have a son, but their daughter might be worth getting to know, according to the report Victoria had before her; *'She is well liked, responsible and, most importantly, her name has never been linked to anyone.'* She was undoubtedly good-looking, and it was likely that some of the men in Seph's life had tried their luck, but none had succeeded in ruining her reputation. It was undoubtedly sound, so no meat for the press.

The Grant house was not far from the avenue where Seph lived. Driving up the hill, passing the solidly built, impressively large houses, Seph wondered if the Grants' would be one of them, but it was half-a-mile beyond and even more impressive than the houses she had admired on the way

As she turned into the open gates and parked on the widest part the drive, beyond the double garage, she had no idea that Victoria was watching her from the wide bay window of the study. Seph would not have worried; she had taken more care than usual about what she wore. The pencil slim skirt of her dark blue suit was flattering, and she had chosen to wear with it a cream, roll-neck blouse.

She wore a minimum of jewellery, but the heavy Lapis lazuli pendant and matching earrings took the edge off the severity of the suit. She would look even less formal when she removed her jacket to reveal the soft flowing, bishop sleeves of the blouse.

Taking a deep breath Seph rang the front door bell. After a phone call from Margot earlier, making sure she knew the location of their house, she now knew enough about the job offered, to hope that she would get it. It sounded attractive and lucrative ...accompanying her son – all expenses paid – every weekend for at least two months. As a PA she would need to manage appointments – ensuring that things went smoothly and that contact details for anyone of note were not lost. The thought that kept nagging at her was that there had to be more to it than that!

She would soon find out; Margot, smiling warmly, was opening the front door.

Revelations

Sitting at her desk on Sunday evening, Seph's head was still spinning. In the two hours she'd spent with Margot, not only had she accepted the job offered but, in the last few minutes, when it was impossible to back out without being rude, she had also experienced serious misgivings.

At first, after accepting tea and sandwiches, Seph learned with astonishment about her own grandfather being a friend of Margot's mother, long ago, in Singapore. It was fascinating to hear more of the background to his life and Margot did not doubt that she would hear a lot more from Victoria, who was looking forward to meeting her.

When Margot eventually spoke about the PA job, she added very little to what she'd said already except that it would be a great help to her son. It would start with a weekend in

Oxford and Seph should be ready to leave on Friday afternoon.

It was obviously a dream of a job, which any girl would eagerly accept, so Seph couldn't resist asking why only she would be asked – after all, it was more pleasurable than difficult. Margot hesitated for a moment and then asked, "Have you read any of my son's books?"

"I'm sorry, I confess I didn't even know that your son was an author, although I am aware that your mother has written several and I would like to have read one, but they seem to be out of print." Seph felt slightly uncomfortable but Margot was not disconcerted.

"I'm not in the least surprised you haven't come across Daniel's," Margot said. "They are well written, and funny, but not books that I imagine would be your first choice from a shelf. However, I will give you a few to read before Friday – then you will be better equipped to deal with him."

The way she said it set alarm bells ringing but Seph had no doubt that she could cope.

As if reading her thoughts, Margot shook her head and tried to explain... "Daniel usually travels alone and although he survives, he gets really stressed. Every young female within miles targets him and some are not easy to get rid of. He's not naturally discourteous and finds it hard to be rude to anyone, plus, it wouldn't do his image any good either."

She tried to make this last point seem of minor importance and continued by saying that he flatly refused to invite any of his female acquaintances to go with him. Everyone, including the girl, would consider them to be 'an item' and he would be trapped into a relationship, however superficial.

Seph could appreciate the problem but asked why she fell into a different category. The answer shocked her. She'd never suspected that her background and conduct had been under scrutiny for several months; she had to control her instinctive outrage.

Margot was aware of the effect of her words but said that only by convincing herself that she'd found the right girl could she keep faith with her son. He had agreed to accept a travelling companion chosen by his mother, on condition that she came with a guarantee that she didn't expect *any* extra-curricular activity – he valued his privacy when not on duty.

"I don't mean that Daniel is in any way unfriendly, but he's been pursued by too many young women who think that they can change him from a misogynist to a lover... I hope they will give up, if they think he's found someone already."

Seph could see her point, but the thought of working with a woman-hater was not very appealing. Margot was quick to reassure her that she had exaggerated, but Daniel formed his poor opinion of the opposite sex at an early age.

He had later witnessed the turmoil in both his brothers' lives caused by their wives' extravagance and this made him even more intransigent.

Seph was slightly reassured. She had come across several marriages that sounded similar, and single males who only saw the worst in women. She had never felt the slightest urge to reform them and she was not likely to start with Daniel. She'd taken to heart all the advice against marrying an unsuitable man, thinking that he could be changed – it never worked.

If anyone ever married her, hoping to change her, she would resent it bitterly and hate them for it. If they were unable to love her, faults and all, they should leave her alone.

Seph's rambling thoughts were brought back to the present abruptly when she realised that Margot was leaving the room. What had she just said? Something about her mother... It came back to her now: Victoria believed that if the granddaughter of Martin Montague had inherited even half his sterling character, she would be a perfect choice.

Within a few moments, Margot returned. "I've just told my mother that you've accepted our proposition, so she's gone to tell Daniel and, when she has clarified the situation for him, will bring him here to meet you." Seeing Seph's expression she laughed, "He agreed several weeks ago to accept my choice, but has probably forgotten, thinking I would fail to find anyone I liked. How wrong he was!"

With her journal open in front of her, Seph read again her account of the afternoon. At the point it ended, she had been lost for words, just as she had been when Victoria joined them with her grandson. Picking up her pen, she tried again...

Margot and I were standing near the door, where she was showing me a portrait of her mother painted fifty years ago. She was beautiful and as Victoria entered and I turned to meet her, my first thought was that there were still traces of the girl in her, despite her age.

The tall, broad shouldered, young man who had pushed open the door, allowing her to come in first, followed and turned to shut it, so my first sight of him was of his back. His waist and hips seemed incredibly narrow.

I noted that, although he had apparently not been expecting company, his shirt and trousers looked immaculate. It was good to know that I wouldn't have to dress down in my working hours, but nothing prepared me for what I felt when he faced me and looked down into my eyes.

Knowing that everyone was watching, waiting for my reaction, I steeled myself to stay calm and smile as Victoria took my hand

and then introduced Daniel to me. We shook hands politely and he indicated that we should sit on the settee together.

I looked away from him to hear, from her own lips, how Victoria had met my grandfather and I told her how sad I was that I had no memory of my father's parents. She promised to show me photographs of them.

I avoided looking at Daniel again, but could feel his eyes on me and wondered what he was thinking, immediately wanting him to like me...

I hoped nobody could read my mind, I'd be fired before I started, and this job was beginning to look more interesting!

His looks alone would probably not have thrown me off balance – I have occasionally been 'wowed', but there was something disturbingly penetrating in his amazingly blue eyes when they met mine.

He has a quiet confident manner, and already I know that working alongside him is going to be more difficult than I thought. I will have to be on guard constantly against showing how smitten I am!

I keep re-living every second we were together... feeling elated and anxious at the same time. I don't believe in love at first sight – at least, I don't think I do – time will tell, but the man is the definition of sexy, I don't think it matters what his books are like.

Daniel's image and the sound of his voice won't leave my head, and I might well regret my promise to avoid becoming an ardent member of his fan club ...but I will certainly make sure that none of the others gets too close!

Family Ties

Over their evening meal, when Seph tried to describe her new position as PA to a successful author, it was impossible to hide the fact that Daniel Grant had made an impression on her. Continually referring to him as her employer didn't distance him enough to deceive her mother, who sat looking happily smug, casting glances full of not very well-hidden meaning at her father.

He feigned not to notice and was much more interested in hearing of things his father had done before his return to England in 1952. He'd rarely spoken about his early days in the army and, when he did, it was usually to answer his questions about jungle warfare.

Martin Montague had loved the tropical rainforests and all the creatures that flourished beneath the huge jungle canopies, in the steamy heat. He never tired of describing the comforting night-noises or the eerie alarming silence when they suddenly stopped.

When any threat struck fear into the heart of the forest, every creature's breath was held until the danger passed. Soldiers under canvas would tense with each momentary silence; was an enemy patrol sneaking up on their camp? ...Or was a four-legged prowler seeking its prey? Being on patrol in a jungle, night or day, was an unforgettable experience.

After dinner, as Seph helped to clear the table, her mother couldn't resist asking for more details about Daniel but Seph didn't want to give an opinion on either his looks or his personality. Seph handed her one of his books.

"His mother says I will have a better understanding of him if I read the kind of things he writes. She gave me a heap of books. Apparently, his opinion of women is unbelievably low, so I'd better look through them and digest before he collects me on Friday."

When Jill re-joined Jack carrying a coffee tray, she was smiling, and he had no doubt why. "Just because this young man seems to have made an impression on our usually '*immune to male charms*' daughter – don't get your hopes up. Seph's only a kid yet, plenty of time to settle down. Let her enjoy herself."

"Oh, you," she retorted, "you're like all fathers – you don't think any boy walking is good enough for your daughter! You must admit, this one is promising – and even has a connection with the family."

Seph heard them as she went upstairs and immediately remembered that she wanted to talk to Dion about this family connection! He must have known about it ...he'd been with their Grandparents for more years than she had existed yet had claimed to know nothing about Margot.

Before starting to read the first of the five books of Daniel's that she had been given, 'The Only Way Is Hers' Seph decided to jot down a few lines in her Daybook. Several remarks Dion had made as she drove to the Grants' house, now had more significance...

I asked him if he had discovered anything about the job on offer and he said it didn't

matter, which annoyed me. "It matters to me,"
I told him, and he said he was sure I wouldn't
care this time tomorrow. "I thought you said
you couldn't see into the future," I reminded
him. He didn't need to, he smiled, because he
knew about the past.

As usual, when we were working up to an
interesting argument, he distracted me by
saying that another film about heaven was on
tonight. It was in Hong Kong and he wanted
to have a good look around, so he would have
to wait until tomorrow to hear what happened
at my interview.

"How did you find out about the film then?"
I asked.

"Looked it up, of course," he said
dismissively. He'd Googled 'Heaven+film title'
and it hadn't taken long to find one still
showing. He raised his eyebrows and added
informatively that it came up with twenty-
three million, seven hundred-thousand titles
in twenty-three seconds.

Despite my previous irritation, I had to
smile. He takes worldly ways in his stride and
is a very fast learner. His eagerness to

experience as much as he can during his time here on earth is endearing ...and the very thought upsets me; how would I bear to lose him again?

"Whose computer have you been messing about with?" I asked, knowing he would not have entered the house ...but I should have guessed: the internet cafe, where else?

Because of my (understandable but I think unusual) interest in the subject, I have read a lot of books about psychic stuff in the last few years. It should be easy to check with Dion whether the experiences are likely to be genuine, but it isn't. He shrugs indifferently, more eager to get answers to his own questions.

Now, thinking about Hong Kong, I told him about some people being able to travel in Spirit and jokingly asked if he could take me with him. He didn't quite get my point and looked at me with unmistakeable scorn... "What a silly question," he said, "I'm not Harry Potter!"

Stung by his tone and aware that I shouldn't have tried to be funny, I could not *hold back my quick retort... "You lied then – you do watch films other than those about heaven – even fairy stories." Can the face of a ghost pale? I think it did, and he disappeared abruptly.*

There was no time to worry about his possibly hurt feelings then, because the house was in sight and when I left it, I was not thinking too clearly about anything, but I do need to talk to Dion about our Grandpa Martin.

In fact, I'm not so much worried about Dion's hasty departure, as eager to learn more about the grandparents I have never known. I must talk more to my Dad about his family.

Thinking about the family, it troubles me that although Dion accepts me as his sister, he shows no desire to be closer to our mum and dad. If they knew he was near, they would want us all to be together. I'd be happier too if he sat about with us sometimes – watching TV – or went with Dad to football matches or to play golf. It has been troubling me for some time and I now have the answer.

Finishing her account at this point, Seph put away her journal and went into the garden. Dion might be in Hong Kong, but he would know she was sitting on the rockery steps, where they used to play together, and he would soon come to her. Grandma had told him never to go where he was not invited so that's what she would do – he belonged in their home as much as she did, and she knew him well enough now, to be confident that he would not do anything to alarm or offend...

Less than five minutes later Dion was sitting by her side, but he was far too excited to listen to her when she tried to speak about her own latest thoughts.

"Tell me later," he interrupted, *"you have to listen – you'll never guess where I've been tonight!"* Without waiting for her to say, 'watching a film in Hong Kong', he told her... *"I've been to a Neighbourhood Watch meeting in the village and we have a job to do."*

It took a while to calm him down but eventually she put together the whole story. The film had been so boring that he explored the island instead. He enjoyed the ferry trip to Kowloon and watched people playing mah-jong until the noisy shuffling of the tiles (*'the twittering of the sparrows'),* and hysterically happy din of hundreds of people enjoying their night out, drove him away. He was passing the Church Hall, *"on my way home,"* he said ...and this filled Seph with pleasure; he really did regard this tiny spot in the whole universe as 'home'.

There were people hurrying into the hall, which was already half-full, so he joined them to find out what was happening. The doors closed immediately, and the meeting started – it was all about letting the police know if strangers were acting suspiciously.

The idea appealed to him and he was so absorbed that when a latecomer arrived and sat next to him, he barely noticed. Dion had taken an aisle seat on an empty row at the back and if the man had sat on his lap he would not have been as surprised as he was when he suddenly realised that the man had excused himself for passing between him and the speaker. In every lull, they conversed... Whoever it was had no idea that to everyone else he must have appeared to be talking to himself!

This aspect of his encounter didn't bother Dion. It was what he discovered that he wished to tell Seph. His new friend told him that several houses had been burgled and the most recent was in the next road to theirs ...so the thief was getting closer and this was their opportunity to help the police again. All she had to do was to be ready to go out and be a witness to the break-in, day or night.

"And what possible excuse would I give for leaving my warm bed in the middle of the night to witness, by sheer chance, a burglary in progress?" Seph asked, trying to be patient.

"You'll think of something, I know. It will be fun – you'll see – and you'll become famous as a private ear."

"You mean 'eye', a private detective, although ear in this case is quite appropriate! It is highly commendable that you want to fight crime, but I don't want you throwing stones at my window or bellowing at me from the garden in the middle of the night." Seeing his face crumple with disappointment, she offered a compromise.

"I will consider helping at any time between eight in the mornings and midnight. In the small hours, you'll have to cope alone. Couldn't you just follow them and get their address, or watch where they store their loot?" It was beginning to strike her as a good idea too ...if only she could find enough ingenious explanations for her many coming successes at striking fear into the heart of the criminal world. Full of enthusiasm, Dion left before Seph had a chance to discuss anything she had intended.

In the quiet of the garden, she relived every moment of her day, still not being able to believe that Daniel Grant might prove more difficult to deal with, than any other male she had ever met.

She must appear outwardly unmoved in her business dealings with him, otherwise she would just become another of the besotted girls he tried to avoid.

Tonight, her bedtime reading might yield some clues about his expectations ...at least, she could only hope!

If you Can't Stand the Heat

On Monday morning, Seph received a frantic text from Shell... Seph was already aware that Letitia Ledbetter, the woman writer from the Book Circle, had rung Shell several times. She had been trying to persuade Shell to visit her to discuss her manuscript. Shell had at last given in, but she wanted Seph to go with her. *"IK ur bz but I promisd we'd b der @ 6pm plz pik me ^"*

Seph couldn't believe it – the nerve of the girl! Her own plan for the day had been to wade through Daniel Grant's books. It was infuriating, but she could not refuse; the idea of letting Shell down never even crossed her mind. One thing she could do, which she had not considered before, was rope Shell into her reading programme!

Of the five books Margot had given her, she had handed the third and fourth to her mother. She opted to keep the first and last and ask Shell to read number two. She would demand a written review of it before the weekend – it was the least Shell could do for ruining her day! In a brief exchange of texts, Shell was delighted to be given the job of reviewer and assured Seph that Letty's place *(they had obviously spoken enough on the phone to become familiar, Seph noted)* was within walking distance of her own house, so ten minutes before the hour would be a good time to be picked up.

Since breakfast she had alternated between reading and writing and been unable to settle seriously to either. Her father worked from home, so after lunch she would have only an hour or two to spare before she needed to go out. Sounds of activity below and the appetizing smells tempted her downstairs.

This might be a good time to chat about the old days – family stuff she'd love to hear. Just how much did her father, Jack, know about

Martin and Pamela Montague? He must know that if Grandma Pamela had not objected, he would have been Christened Dionysus ...and clearly had not been happy to be named Jacob.

Seph was glad her mother had been more amenable to Greek myths. Jill loved all the classics, in literature or music. Perhaps she could steer the conversation round to Dion. She couldn't hide forever from their parents, the fact that he lived on in spirit and was happy and handsome ...but seeing how busy her mother was, it probably not the right time to reveal all.

Had Seph but known, Jill did sometimes think of her first-born child... It was not a loss that still filled her like a solid block of ice – that sorrow had become easier to bear, when she'd realised that she was pregnant again. She'd often felt sad for Seph that fate had deprived her of a brother, but Seph had always made friends easily and Jill soon stopped worrying about her being an only child.

Jack was so thankful that he had not lost his wife as well as their first baby that he refused to wallow in grief.

He mourned, of course, but probably thought that any open display, or discussion, would not help Jill. At her birth, Seph immediately became his pride and joy and even Jill was unsure if he ever thought of their lost son.

When Seph found her mother alone, laying the table. Jill was humming along happily with the radio, which was barely audible in the background. Looking at the three places set, Seph risked asking, "Do you ever wonder what it would have been like cooking for four of us?" The surprise on her mother's face embarrassed Seph briefly and she added hastily, "I mean – Dion might still have been living at home ...and ...do you ever wonder what he would have done – the career he might have chosen?"

Turning away to straighten the chairs, Jill took so long to answer that Seph wished she hadn't asked. Then, to her relief, her mother admitted that she sometimes daydreamed about what might have been. "It was not to be – I faced up to that – but, as the years went by, I pictured him always a little taller than you, the image of your Dad. We have photos of your Dad as a boy, with his parents, so I suppose it was easy to pretend."

"You said he was in Heaven, when you first told me about him," Seph ventured, "Did you ever imagine him looking down on us? Would you like to think he was still part of our family?"

Had she gone too far? Seph held her breath...

Jill answered without hesitation. "He will always be part of me and my family ...as you will always be – wherever you are!" It was as much as Seph could have expected, and she decided to tackle Dion next; how exactly did he feel about his earthly family?

Later, when she drove away to pick up Shell, she grew increasingly impatient when Dion didn't show up. As she braked in front of the house and waved, in answer to Shell, who was at an upstairs window, he startled her by yelling in her ear. *"That's it! They're on their own – I'll never help them again!"*

Nothing he managed to babble between then and the moment Shell joined them, made sense. He did not even hesitate when Shell opened the door and swung herself into the passenger seat. He disappeared and reappeared in the back of the car, still ranting about not being appreciated. The urgency of Seph's mental pleas that they should put off talking about whatever it was, resulted in his leaving abruptly.

Seph was worried – he was over-reacting to every setback these days. She told herself, with fingers crossed, that it couldn't be anything serious, and tried to follow what Shell was telling her about Letty Ledbetter.

"She is really quite nice, but weird. She can't understand why her manuscript is full of mistakes because she checks it on the computer. It's obvious that she follows every suggestion that the word processor throws up, indiscriminately! Pathetic!"

It seemed that the object of their visit was to hear the highlights of Letty's life story. She wanted to be sure that she was tackling it in the most interesting way possible.

Shell was so wound up about the responsibility of advising Letty that she kept forgetting to issue directions, so the ten-minute drive took twenty.

Letty was waiting at the gate to greet them and invited them in, smiling happily, even though they were late.

Every time they'd made a U-turn, Dion appeared briefly in Seph's driving mirror, with a huge grin on his face, so Seph glared at him as she locked the car. Thank goodness, she thought, he would not follow them inside. Although the afternoon was still comfortably warm, there was a fire in the sitting room and when their hostess left, to put the kettle on, they both moved as far away from it as possible and stared at it, lost for words.

At either side of the fireplace were two sleeping cats, and while Seph was wondering if they were alive or stuffed, another suddenly jumped onto her lap. Her shriek of alarm caused one of the others to open its eyes. Its companion remained undisturbed, mainly because it really did turn out to be stuffed. An aroma of cats filled the air and together with the heat, they both began to feel sick.

Shell moved around the room like a caged animal and pointed out the dozens of photographs on every surface: all were of cats! "There isn't a speck of dust in here, although the grate is filled with ash from burnt logs – but how can she stand the heat – and she's obviously potty about cats," she said.

Seph did not know whether to be pleased or sorry when their hostess, within a few minutes of returning, realised how uncomfortably warm they were and suggested going out into the garden. After the first wave of relief, she realised that Dion might join them, but after an hour had passed and there had been no sign of him, Seph managed to become genuinely interested in Letty's adventures and relaxed until, suddenly, Letty raised her eyes from the chapter she was reading and was so startled by what she saw that she screamed hysterically several times before collapsing into a weeping heap.

It was an afternoon Seph would never forget.

Good Intentions

Seph was too exhausted after returning home to be able to concentrate on reading anything, let alone any of Daniel Grant's books. She wanted to be fully in control of her critical capacity when assessing their content... Just how much of a woman-hater was he? More than likely it was just a pose – just a gimmick to sell his books. Her mind was too occupied with the events at Letty's to relax, so she decided to update her diary...

The discussion with Letty went well until Dion interfered... We were in the garden, never having been out of Letty's sight – and immediately prior to leaving the three cats in the sitting room, Letty had pointed at the one that was stuffed and was almost in tears recounting how devoted a pet Lulu had been – the little darling had followed her everywhere, couldn't bear her to be out of sight.

So, as we sat outside, you can imagine the look of horror on her face when she looked up and saw the stuffed Lulu swaying gently on the branch of a nearby tree.

Shell was equally stunned but didn't scream and shriek as loudly as their hostess.

I didn't need to wonder who was responsible. We didn't stay long after that but thank goodness we were not in the firing line when blame started flying. Those 'dreadful children next door' were first in line ...but what could I say? I was furious with Dion; how could he have been so crass?

As soon as Shell was dropped off I tackled him. "I thought you didn't enter where you were not invited – and what possessed you to move the stuffed cat to the tree?"

Dion looked stunned at my outburst, but the 'little boy lost' look wasn't going to work with me... He protested that we'd all been invited in together when we arrived. The fact that Letty couldn't see him, apparently, didn't occur to him!

*"I saw the cat sniffing at its own dead fur,"
he said, "and tried to make it understand that
the lady would love to know that her darling
Lulu was still about, but the stupid cat didn't
understand me. I tried to show the silly
creature that it should sit in the tree."* Dion
sighed heavily and said he was sorry – he had
only tried to help.

I couldn't decide whether he was being
mischievous or had really thought that seeing
the ghost of her pet haunting the garden
would comfort her, let alone a stuffed one, but
her shrieking had terrified him.

He just kept repeating that he'd had
enough of trying to help people ...which
reminded me that I still didn't know what had
upset him earlier.

Putting her memoirs aside, she went out to sit
near the rockery, hoping he would join her in
a better mood than when they'd parted. The sun
had set, and the air was cooling rapidly, but he
still didn't appear, so she gave up and, feeling
more than a little worried about what he was
up to. She returned to the house, where her

parents greeted her, obviously eager for news of her day.

Her carefully edited version of events made them happy and they were pleased that Shell had found something so interesting and useful to do; they knew how Seph worried about her shyness.

It wasn't difficult to bring up the subject of their being, ostensibly, both without siblings and Jack went so far as to say how sad it was for them to have lost Dion at birth. He took Jill's hand and kissed it before looking at Seph with a sad smile. "We like to think he is still with us, with his brotherly eye on you, keeping you safe."

Recollecting the conversation she'd overheard years ago, Seph knew they must have sensed that her childhood friend was Dion and it would please them to be in her confidence. For now, perversely, she hugged the knowledge to herself ...but soon, when she could rely on Dion being on his best behaviour, she would tell them, confident that they would be comfortable with his presence, whether they could see him or not.

A Wanted Man

After dinner with her parents Seph excused herself saying that, rather than watch TV, she would have an early night and read in her room. They would probably be happy to have some time together, she thought, and they understood anyway that she wanted to read her new employer's books.

The titles of the books indicated that they were about the same main character, although they were not in any particular order. "Great Escapes" was the name of the series and number one was "Ed the Babysitter". It was a second edition, so all five books were listed: "Ed Takes a Fall", "Ed in Trouble", "Ed at Sea" and the fifth was "Ed Breathes Again".

They were all short novels …about 220 pages, which she guessed was less than 45,000 words. None would take too long to read, which was probably part of their appeal. *Not exactly weighty tome stuff,* she thought – then immediately chided herself. She was already regarding his fans with antagonism... *Surely, she couldn't be jealous; she hardly knew Daniel Grant*‼

Perversely, Seth opened book five, wanting to know how the series ended – happy or 'in the air', leaving an opportunity for more 'Ed' books. As she read, she couldn't shake off the feeling that she was picturing Daniel as 'Ed' and imagining that Ed's thoughts and words were what Daniel would have said in similar circumstances. The character was never discourteous or rude to any of his female acquaintances – but he didn't seem to like any of them.

In a way, she could understand why his female readers would believe that Ed was Daniel's mouthpiece and each one felt challenged. Even had he not been so attractive, his success would have made him a target anyway. The fact that he was so, *sooo*, handsome ...well! Seph suddenly snapped the book shut, aware that she must not allow herself to have any feelings at all for Daniel.

Not only would she lose her peach of a job but, worse, she might never see him again...

Too unsettled to resume reading, Seph decided to go into the garden for some fresh air and, of course, hoping Dion would turn up. She really wanted to know what had upset him and who was it that he wouldn't try to help in future...

Her parents were still watching TV, so she peered through the open door to tell them where she was going – she didn't want to be locked out when they went to bed! Her father offered her a glass of wine to take out with her, which she accepted, and her mother pointed out a headline in the local paper; a four-year-old boy was missing from his home in their neighbourhood. The stricken family lived a few minutes' walk away on an adjacent road, but they didn't know them...

As Seph sat under a sky bright with stars, gazing across the still garden, she couldn't help thinking that she should not have been so dismissive when Dion was keen to police the nearby streets.

The only sounds were of far distant traffic

and the closer hooting of an owl, but within a few minutes she heard Dion's voice before he materialised – he'd decided it was less startling if other people were with her. It pleased her to know that he was becoming more aware of the fact that there could be others, apart from Seph, who sensed his presence and might even see him.

It might have been less startling had he not sounded hysterically loud!

"He's done it again!"

"Who has done what again?" I asked

The 'he' turned out to be the man who had unexpectedly seen and spoken with Dion at the meeting the other night and apparently still had no idea that he was an apparition. They had walked away from the meeting discussing how they could 'take turns' observing the road that the burglars seemed to be targeting.

The following night they met at midnight and Charlie hadn't endeared himself by using Dion's full name to reprimand him.

"Dionysus Montague, you are five minutes late!"

"I could have told him I was in a different

time zone when I remembered that I'd agreed to meet him, but didn't think that a lonely road on a dark night was a good moment to say I was a ghost... I hate that word. Why can't you give me another name for being undead?"

"To me, you are a spirit," said Seph, "and a very lively one... Who called you a ghost? You haven't exactly a huge circle of friends on earth!"

"Your friend, Fishy, said the cat-lady looked as if she'd seen a ghost – and I knew it was a cat – so I googled it."

Seph sighed. "My friend is Shell – Sheila really, so it's a good job she'll never hear you calling her Fishy ...but what did you learn from Google – and whose machine did you use this time?"

"I first found a Gost Girl on You Tube, but soon saw that almost all the others were either surnames or spelled with an 'h' – ghosts – so I wasn't the only one who didn't know how to spell it." After a moment's thought he said, *"I'm usually good. When I was very little, Grandma said Constantinople is a very easy word and asked me to spell it."*

"I bet you said, 'I T' at your first try!" Seph raised one eyebrow.

When Dion had tried several times to copy her brow-lift, and failed, he at last answered.

"Yes. I did – I've always been very literal …and it was at the police station – the PCs' PC you might say…" He giggled, then resumed hastily. *"I went back there when you were so angry with me, to find out if there had been any more burglaries near us."*

Seph suddenly felt very mean and was sorry to have upset him so much, but still hadn't heard what happened later to make him angry. Who was it he had tried and failed to help?

At last he went back to describe his vigil with Charles Trevor Basil Biggs-Brown. It was the length of his name when Charlie introduced himself that had prompted Dion to give his own in full, but Dion had not appreciated Charlie's tone of voice when he delivered his complaint about the time.

"He reminded me of some of the men in that pub when our murderer was arrested," Dion said indignantly, *"he swayed about a lot and his voice was funny."*

Charlie left him, promising to return in four hours. In his absence, Dion had seen something highly suspicious and been unable to do anything about it, but at least he had memorised a car number plate, which he gave to Charlie as soon as he came back. *"Instead of being pleased, he was furious, and told me I should have called the police."* Dion hesitated before admitting, *"So I shouted at him 'Do it yourself and disappeared."*

Seph hardly dared ask what Charlie had done, but Dion continued. *"He thought I must have run to the back of the house, and he went to look. When he saw the back door open he peeped inside to see if I was there – but before he could say anything, a woman came out and hit him with a frying pan – then her husband appeared and said he had called the police and they tied Charlie up while he was still on the ground."*

Dion tagged along when the police took Charlie away. They heard from him about the plan to protect the neighbourhood and he gave them the registration number of the car Dion saw. *"He gave them my name and description too, so now I'm a wanted man!"* Dion moaned, *"And Charlie won't talk to me because I said I can't talk to the police. He doesn't understand."*

It was clear to Seph that she should find Charlie, but Dion was adamant that she must not. Charlie was his responsibility and he, not Seph, would deal with him. Seph, knowing how mischievous Dion could be, was concerned that Charlie might have a weak heart – goodness only knew what her inventive brother would devise, so she made Dion promise to confront Charlie only when she was around to see the encounter.

Before he vanished again – he was anxious to see another film about Heaven, which was about to be shown at a foreign language festival in Singapore – Seph asked him if he knew that a local toddler was missing. He did, and that led to another tirade.

Dion was in the police station when the report came in and, having spent hours watching the road they mentioned, he was sure the boy hadn't been kidnapped. At the beginning of his watch he had seen a small child walk alone across the road and into another garden, so it might be the one they had lost. He went straight back to see what was happening and saw a police car in the drive of the house that the child had left. Other policemen and women were walking from house to house, asking questions.

The garden that Dion saw the child enter was not large and, at a glance, he saw nowhere he could be hiding. Somehow, he sensed that the boy had gone through the hedge, so he followed, into the adjacent garden to the road beyond. Following his instinct again, after looking up and down, he crossed over and entered another open gate.

At the back of the property, several children were playing. A small table held the remnants of what must have been a tea-party. A few sandwiches and cakes remained. Dion watched, knowing the missing boy was close but not sure whether he could be one of those at the party.

Eventually a woman appeared, and they were all ushered inside. Dion reasoned that she would have noticed if one had been a stranger, so he looked inside a garage and a garden-shed

– delighted to see he had been right. There, fast asleep on some sacking among the tools, was the child. Seph was pleased and eager to hear how Dion had let everyone know where he could be found.

"That's why I'm so angry," Dion almost shouted. *"When I went back to the station there was a very weird woman. I overheard that she was going into a trance and would then describe the kidnapper. Everyone was just watching her, and she didn't get up to go anywhere."*

He stopped to shake his head, quite mystified, not knowing that she was a local character who claimed to be psychic. *"Then she suddenly opened her eyes and looked straight at me and pointed her finger and told everyone that I was the one who had taken the boy."* Dion kept trying to tell her that she was wrong, but she was too busy describing him to anyone who would listen.

No wonder he was upset and wanted to wash his hands of the whole affair – but Seph had to persuade him that they couldn't let the boy spend another night in a shed. Dion laughed when she said that the child must be hungry… He had already thought of that and had wrapped all the cakes and sandwiches in paper napkins then dropped them in through a window. Inside, he'd placed them where the child would see them as soon as he woke up.

Following directions, Seph drove to get the address of the house where the child was, according to Dion, fast asleep again. Calling from a telephone box, she informed the police that she had seen a small boy go into the property but not seen him leave.

The shed door may have been open when the child went in but, having closed, the latch was too high for him to open it again; had it not been for Dion, who now glowed under her appreciative comments about his powers of observation, he might not have been found for days.

So, it was a mollified and much calmer Dion who went off to enjoy his film. Seph too was happy until his last comment floated back from a distance as he hurried away…

"Don't worry, I'll deal with Charlie when I get back…"

Big Bro's Busy Night

An update appeared in the local paper, the following night, congratulating the police on finding the lost infant so quickly, but news travels quickly and the only thing not already known was that an anonymous caller had tipped them off.

The report explained that the boy had wandered into the property and seen all the party food. Quite understandably he had been tempted to eat some of the pretty cakes. Hearing the partygoers coming out to enjoy the feast he had taken a few goodies with him to the shed, where he fell asleep. It was a shame really, Seph thought; with a little more time to plan, it might have been an opportunity to enhance her reputation as a detective… On the other hand, a lost child was not something to exploit.

Seph was way behind with all the reading she had planned to do before Friday but found it difficult to concentrate. "Ed Breathes Again" was not gripping; her mind strayed constantly, wondering, literally, where in the world Dion was. She must ask him if their grandparents ever nipped down to see him; perhaps he had made enough progress with his earthly studies by now to be allowed to visit them again…

After less than ten minutes into reading Daniel's book, it was clear already that Ed could not be mistaken for a hero. Described as below average height, and plump enough to huff and puff after climbing the steps to his own front porch, he did not sound attractive and his over-gelled spiked hair, being ginger, could not have helped. Had his hair been described as red-gold it would have sounded like a saving grace, but it was perfectly obvious that Daniel did not like Ed, his own main character.

Despite all his shortcomings, Ed was never

deprived of female company and it soon became obvious just how much Daniel scorned womankind.

Ed's great magnet was his wealth.

He was, in fact, a brainy boffin who had invented a couple of computer apps in his teens.

By the time he reached twenty, he'd settled his parents and grandparents in country cottages in Yorkshire and financed the husbands of his two older sisters so that they were running businesses, placing them near enough to the oldies never to be short of baby-sitters. The new business that his father started, using his son's money, was immensely successful, but with success came an underlying resentment that he had needed his son to help him. Family divisions fractured his parents' relationship and they went through a bitter divorce as his father fought to keep his newly acquired wealth.

Ed's own property was a good distance away, in Oxfordshire – an imposing mansion on the river Thames. with a boathouse for his cruiser at the bottom of the garden,

Ed's male followers were always ready to party and eager to 'befriend' any female who needed to be consoled because Ed had not chosen her. It was evident, a couple of hours into reading the book that Daniel accepted the men's behaviour as normal; what else could women expect if they shamelessly pursued a chap, simply because he was well off!

Seph didn't need to read more so skipped on, nearer to the end...

...Poor Ed had drunk more than was good for him one night, although it was hinted that the unscrupulous young girl had spiked his drinks before climbing into bed with him. As she managed to video-call half the county before dawn, he was almost trapped into marriage!

At last, the final chapter...

"Ed breathed again when her father accepted a considerable amount of cash to find a way to stop the marriage.

Knowing his daughter well, George had already decided that marrying Ed would be a mistake, not that he was going to tell Ed that he had already started trying to break them up. He had a better prospect for her and he was happy be able to double this extra windfall at the dog-track!"

Needing little persuasion, Ed's girl dumps him and marries his wealthy father instead... She ruins the older man, who is forced to move out of luxury to a tiny cottage. Wracked with guilt, Ed tries to save him, losing most of his own wealth, to her machinations, in the process. All the staff in the big house are sacked, though Ed does his best to help them. When the housekeeper's pretty niece helps her to pack and move out of the property – she meets and falls in love with the now penniless Ed, who, by the end of the book, fortunately inherits a trust from distant cousin and is not only able to rescue his Father from penury but can live happily ever after, in style, with a wife who loves him for himself.

A predictable, trite ending... Seph couldn't say she thought it was a good story, but, to be fair, she hadn't read the whole book. She was looking forward to hearing what Shell thought of the one she was reading. The important thing was that Daniel apparently regarded a loving marriage as a happy ending. She regarded it as a sign that he must concede that some women must be lovable ...or was she kidding herself?

Her mother was halfway through hers and said that although not the genre she favoured, she found it interesting enough to finish. She shook her head and warned Seph, "The author's opinion of the female sex is certainly not high."

Seph picked up the newspaper again before going to bed and glanced at the front-page headlines...

An incident outside a local pub caught her eye, for no particular reason; another brawl – so what? The elderly man, who was escorted away by two policemen, was pictured, trying to fight them off and pointing angrily to the post-box on the otherwise empty pavement. According to the report he kept shouting at it, "Tell them – you know it wasn't me! Tell them for God's sake!"

She knew who the man must be; Charlie – she would bet on it. He must be looking at Dion, who was invisible to the camera and to everyone else. She had a feeling that her big brother was not having a good night!

It was an hour later that Dion returned to the rockery below her window. She had been reading for a while and was on the verge of falling asleep when she felt his presence. He must want to talk to her but knew he shouldn't disturb her – he had learned to be thoughtful and would wait until she awoke in the morning. It was no good – she couldn't ignore him. She would have been foolhardy to go outside so late, when her parents were asleep, so this seemed a good time to invite him into the kitchen, where she could legitimately be making herself a hot drink.

When she asked him if he would like to join her in the kitchen, Dion was a little hesitant. *"Are you sure they wouldn't mind?"* he asked, looking hopeful. Seph repeated what their mother had said and added that she felt it was time that she spoke of him and explained how they'd always communicated with each other. He appeared beside her instantly but said he would only come again when he was sure they wanted him.

Seph admired his principles, so didn't protest. Instead she showed him the evening paper and asked what he could do to get Charlie out of trouble. To her astonishment he smiled and said he had the situation under control. He looked so smug, she could have slapped him! "So, start by telling me who accused him of what and how can you tell anybody?"

Dion looked suitably chastened and explained. They were standing at the bar when a pug-ugly guy punched Charlie in the ribs. *Where does he pick up words like pug-ugly Seph wondered...* Charlie turned around and thumped him back, muttering something about not even knowing his wife!

Dion had seen the man earlier, standing at the counter near a charity collection box – and suddenly realised that it had gone. While he was wondering, a fight broke out and fists were flying everywhere.

The police arrived within minutes and 'Pug-ugly' said he'd seen Charlie steal the charity box, which was then found in the deep pocket of Charlie's overcoat, so the poor man was dragged to the lock-up.

"So how are things under control? What have you done to get him out?"

"That will happen tomorrow, when Pug-ugly goes to confess to framing him." Dion, looking even more self-satisfied than before, stopped laughing, at last, and described how he had followed the bully home and started haunting him. Since they had spoken last about heaven and hell, Dion had learned how fearful the living are, of being condemned for eternity to the fires of hell when they die, although never quite believing in it. Why would they? Most don't believe there's a heaven either. While still at the bar, Dion had whispered in his ear, *"YOU ARE EVIL... Evildoers rot in Hell."*

The man whipped round expecting someone to be at his elbow, but the crowd had thinned. Looking shaken and uncertain, he made his way to the door. *"Rot in Hell... Hell... Hell... You are evil... evil... evil..."* Whispers echoed in his ears as he fled.

Ignoring the barman who shouted that his glass was still full, the shaken bully made his way home. Dion tormenting him all the way, describing the heat and flames, fanned by the devil, and the evildoers whose backs were breaking as they fed fuel to the flames.

Still not really believing that he could be hearing anything 'out of this world', he filled his kettle at the sink ...he needed to sober up, that was it... the booze. He ignited the gas under the kettle and shook with fright as the flame went out and the kettle rose and emptied itself into the sink. Still convinced he was hallucinating, he gave up and prepared for bed. It was no use – Dion whispered, non-stop, about the suffering he would have to endure if he didn't confess that he had framed Charlie unjustly, for no good reason.

Dion said that he shouted his reasons – something about Charlie stealing his wife. Dion added that he had checked with Charlie, still locked in a cell, and it wasn't true. She had flirted with him, but he wasn't tempted, she was no catch, and she ran off with someone else ...someone not as fussy, he had added!

Seph suggested that he might change his mind in the morning, but one look at Dion's wide grin convinced her that it wasn't likely. One other thing puzzled her... "Presumably," she said, "you visited Charlie in jail. "Didn't he wonder how you got in? He surely must know that the police wouldn't have allowed him to have a visitor."

"He was too pleased to see me but couldn't understand why I hadn't spoken up for him when he was arrested."

"You really will have to tell him that you are invisible to most people. Please let me help you with that."

It was getting late and she urged him to come and tell her in the morning as soon as 'Pug-ugly' had confessed – she was eager to know every detail.

Dion went away happy. He had felt completely at home inside the house and hoped his parents wouldn't mind his floating in and out ...but of course, they would have to invite him first...

The Time Has Come...

Her parents couldn't help feeling concerned about Seph's new job. They were intrigued to hear more about the family connection so Seph seized the opportunity to introduce Dion into the conversation.

"Daniel's grandma thinks Dad must be unhappy not to have been christened Dion himself, and that is why you gave the name to your son. Is that right?"

Her father nodded and said he'd never liked his name or forgiven his mother for saddling him with it. "At Bible class in junior school we learned that Jacob (re-named Israel) wrestled with God and forced God to bless him and I came in for some stick from mates! Shortening

Jacob to Jack made me feel more comfortable, especially when I met Jill!" He grinned apologetically at her mother, then sighed... "Your brother didn't survive his birth, but we still think of him as Dion."

It was a perfect opening for her, so Seph asked, "Do you remember how I played with my unseen friend when I was three years old?" They both smiled and nodded. "Well, he wasn't in my imagination, he was really with me." Her parents looked at each other, neither knowing what to say, so Seph continued. "He was taller than I was then..." she hesitated, then added, "He is still taller than I am, and looks a lot like Dad, in the old photos I've seen."

They were lost for words, wondering about Seph's sanity.

"He grew up, in spirit Dad, with your parents, and says that Gran told him never to go where he wasn't invited." While they were still numb with shock Seph explained how he had been sent back to learn more about the life he'd missed, so that he could understand and help others who had recently passed on.

Recovering slightly, her mother asked, "So

why hasn't he come to us? Why to you?" Alongside the disbelief ...was she a little hurt that he hadn't appeared to her, his mother?

"You haven't invited him into your home, Mum. I invited him into the kitchen the other day and I know he would like to feel that he is part of our family, but he is bound by Gran's instruction and won't come in without your approval."

"If we are to accept what you're telling us, then of course he's welcome to be here, with us, at any time he likes..."

"We are his family, and that instruction sounds just like my mother, I must say," added Jack.

Seph sent her thoughts to Dion and peered through the curtain to the rockery. Within seconds he was there, and she beckoned to him, mentally repeating what their parents had said. They both watched, wondering what was happening, until Seph turned and told them that he was with them now.

Realising how uncomfortable they must feel - how could they know whether she was speaking the truth or mad as a hatter? She had to do something ...or rather Dion had to! He didn't hesitate, he pulled the curtain aside with a loud swish... "Careful, Dion, you'll pull it off the rail..." she shouted, then looked apologetically at their two stunned parents.

An hour later, when all the crying and questions were over, and they accepted that although they couldn't see him, he would come when they thought of him and otherwise would never invade their privacy. They were happy to know that he was with them in spirit, and not lost forever and, through Seph, they even heard how people they loved still exist on the other side.

"I think perhaps you could read my book now," Seph declared, "You wouldn't have believed any of it before..." They gazed at each other, scarcely able to believe it even now, but they were both happy. It was more than they could ever have dreamed of. Their family felt complete. Breaking the silence, Seph switched the television on and changed the channel. "There's a good Western film starting in a few minutes," she said. "The boys will love it Mum − let's go and make supper."

Acceptance

Jack stared at the television wondering if Dion had really stayed to sit with him – still bemused by everything Seph had told them. He remembered what he had been like at twenty-three and visualised Dion sitting in the armchair opposite. As if in answer to him, a cushion on the settee flopped onto the seat from where it had rested upright on the arm.

With a laugh aloud, Jack nodded happily. "Good enough, son," he said, and settled to watch the film.

In the kitchen, when adding things to the trolley, Jill, still in shock at discovering that her first-born was now with them, wondered aloud if he would be present all the time and, if not, how would they know whether he was or not?

Seph could appreciate that there could be many times when they wouldn't welcome company and did her best to assure her mother that Dion was amazingly sensitive and would know when to absent himself. On the other hand, if she spoke to him, or of him, he would come to her. Seph believed that they would soon become aware, in a strange way, when he was present and when not. Anyway, at the slightest hint that he wasn't welcome, he would leave.

In their absence, Jack found himself thinking of his parents and imagining how they had brought up his son – probably in the same way they had him: always strict, but fair. His father was the one who read to him before he could read himself and immediately he thought of "The adventures of Tom Thumb". He was startled. Where on earth had that sprung from – then smiled. Of course, he would have read the same stories to Dion.

He knew that in some strange way, they were communicating, and the thought comforted him. They really did have their son back.

When they returned with supper and mugs of hot chocolate, Jack was obviously enjoying the film and Dion was happy just watching him and his reactions to the on-screen movie. Seph sat with him on the settee and Jill sat opposite Jack, in the armchair.

It was a relief to have been able to bring Dion home to their parents and have someone with whom she could now speak openly about her wonderful, lovable brother. He might sometimes be exasperating but he always meant well, and she dreaded the time when he would be considered to have learned enough and would have to rise to a higher plane.

Tomorrow was going to be a long day, so Seth excused herself and went to her room. Daniel would be picking her up soon after five-o-clock, tomorrow. As well as packing for the weekend she would devote the afternoon to primping herself up: hair, nails, face. Looking at herself, critically, she sighed... So much to do...

Mentally kicking herself for being stupid, she eventually went to bed, daydreamed and slept.

Problem Solved

Seph woke at seven-thirty on Friday morning and finished her usual chores within an hour. Before she'd finished ironing a couple of her smartest blouses and had barely started packing, she sensed that Dion was waiting for her to go downstairs, so she went to the kitchen to make herself coffee and toast.

He pretended to act casually but she could tell he was pleased with himself and guessed why... "So, all is well then," she said, "...'Pug-Ugly' went to the police and confessed his sins to save his soul?"

"He couldn't get there fast enough," Dion confirmed. *"At first when he woke up, he convinced himself that he'd been drunk and last night was a nightmare, but he began to have second thoughts when he ran water for his bath while he shaved. Turning back to the bath, he discovered that the plug was still*

hanging on the tap."

When Dion stopped laughing he continued...
"When he fled to the kitchen and tried to pick up the kettle, it floated out of reach, and all the time I kept reminding him that he was on his way to Hell and Damnation. 'Liar, liar, liar...' I chanted to him... All the way to the Police Station!"

"So, your friend Charlie is a free man now?" Seph asked, and Dion nodded, but suddenly looked solemn.

"Yes, and he's looking for me. He thinks it's my fault he spent the night in a cell, because I didn't defend him last night."

Seph made up her mind. She had over five hours to get ready for Daniel, so she insisted that Dion give her directions to wherever Charlie was, so that she could clarify the situation for him. Dion didn't argue this time and they were soon on their way to the bar of the *Horse and Hounds.*

Charlie was clutching his glass, looking tired and extremely unhappy. When Seph approached and greeted him with a smile, holding out her hand to shake his, his jaw dropped. "Hello, Charlie. How do you do?" she said, smiling. "I'm Dion's sister."

"Where the hell is he?" Charlie half rose to his feet but flopped back. "He could have put things right last night and saved me an uncomfortable night in gaol."

"That's why I'm here, to explain."

"Too ashamed to come himself then!"

Seph didn't waste time with words but said, He's here. He's sitting at the table with you."

While Charlie was gaping at her as if she were mad, Seph sat and continued to explain. "My brother is in spirit – most people can't see him. You are the only person he's met with whom he can talk, apart from me, so he didn't want to tell you in case you were frightened, and he lost you as a friend."

As her words sank in, Charlie was at first surprised, then he scoffed, "What rubbish! How gullible do you think I am?" He rose to leave, pushing his chair away from the table and at that moment Dion materialised to him, looking extremely anxious. "Good God," muttered Charlie, falling back again onto the chair and almost toppling over.

"You can go now, Sis. Thanks for coming but I know you have things to do..." Dion smiled – he could never have explained as effectively on his own. As it was, Charlie was already recovering and beginning to appreciate the fact that he was psychic.

"I wonder how many other dead people I've seen or even spoken to in my life?

Seph hastened away. She had a feeling that she wouldn't see much of Dion, this weekend. Was she relieved? He was sure to pick up her mixed feelings about Daniel and she could do without his teasing until she sorted herself out.

She needn't have worried, Charlie was already full of suggestions about all the wrongs they could put right, and he knew just where to start!

Seph was barely out of sight when Charlie launched into an alarming list of things they would be able to do together, to set the world to rights.

"Hang on a minute, Charlie, I do have other things to do you know, so let's not go looking for trouble."

"But we can help each other, surely? What

have you got on your agenda for tomorrow?"

When he tried to explain that he'd been sent to earth to learn about life, as he'd missed out on his childhood, Charlie slapped his thigh delightedly. "There you go then! We'll go to the kindergarten tomorrow morning and see what the little ones do."

Realising that it did make some kind of sense – starting from the beginning – and as there was nothing else pressing to worry about, Dion agreed.

While on a roll, Charlie grabbed his jacket from the back of his seat and set off to settle his bill, having apparently been there since lunchtime. Once outside, he pointed to a school building a few hundred yards down the road. "Come on, let's see what the older kids do when they are let out of school."

An hour later, after watching boys' football practice and girls leaping about a netball court, Dion declared himself bored. He had seen some older boys walking away and followed them to a local bar. Within minutes he was back, asking Charlie about drinking at their age.

Now, suddenly fired with enthusiasm, Charlie

almost ran to the local 'Crown and Anchor'... "Those kids are under age and, if they're being served alcohol, there'll be trouble!"

The bartender looked up in alarm as Charlie hurtled through the swing doors and stood staring around the room, which, at this time in the afternoon, was almost empty. Unsure of his ground, Charlie took a stool at the bar and ordered a pint.

There was no sign of the boys so when he'd finished his drink he went to find the rest-room. It was a chance to look around and he saw them in the garden at the back. Asking Dion to check what they were drinking, he returned to the bar and ordered another pint. It was so long before Dion joined him that he was well into his third and getting upset.

When Dion did slide onto the stool next to him he had no opportunity to get a word in. Dion was ecstatic and praised Charlie's wisdom in directing him to mix with younger age groups. Saying he needed time to take in all he'd learned he faded away with a smile on his face.

Charlie guessed he had returned to the

garden to continue his education. It didn't take a genius to guess what the teenagers were talking about – he'd been one himself once. Shaking his head sorrowfully he started to make his way out but before he reached the door, Dion appeared briefly to tell him that one of the boys was the landlord's son and they were on soft drinks.

He was sorry to be leaving alone but didn't begrudge Dion opting to stay. The young man had a lot of living to catch up on and there was always tomorrow.

Fingers Crossed

Seph eyed the clock – in less than half-an-hour Daniel would be picking her up. She checked the contents of her briefcase yet again, then went downstairs. When the bell sounded, five minutes early, her mother was chatting on the phone and indicated that she should go...

Daniel carried her suitcase to the boot of the car and hurried to open the passenger door for her... He was obviously pleased to see her, which worried Seph slightly; she hoped she would live up to his expectations. He was already living up to hers!

An hour or so later, when she was eventually inside her hotel room, Seph heaved a sigh of relief. The drive had been uneventful, and the weather was beautiful ...the roads were not too crowded for comfort, and conversation flowed easily. She'd stayed with Daniel as he parked in the hotel's underground carpark and they went up in the lift together to check in.

All the formalities were handled smoothly, and they were shown to their respective rooms by a smart young man, who Daniel tipped for them both. He then opened her door for the boy to take in her luggage and handed the key card to her, with a smile.

"We made the trip in good time, so we have two hours before dinner. Shall we meet in the bar at seven-forty-five?" he asked. "Or, if you prefer, I'll ring you when I go down and you can join me when you're ready. There's no rush." Seph told him that she didn't fancy sitting in the bar unaccompanied, so would appreciate his calling her when he left. He seemed to approve of this and, to her surprise, said he was looking forward to a relaxing evening together before facing the working day tomorrow.

Having unpacked her case and hung up her few clothes, she had a shower, then decided to lie down for an hour. She relaxed, having set the alarm on her mobile in case she slept. She didn't think she would, her mind was in such a whirl.

Surprisingly, Seph did fall asleep and was reluctant to move when the alarm woke her at seven-o-clock. His call came half an hour later, and she decided to take her notebook with her to make it seem more like a business dinner. She was prepared to discuss his books, if he wished, although hadn't decided how to avoid giving an opinion on the content. The challenge was having to avoid looking at him without wanting him to flirt!

Daniel's grandmother had obviously spoken at length to him about her much-admired escort when she was a teenager in Singapore. Seph's grandfather had been a trusted, close friend and being at her side during social and official occasions had, to a large extent, educated her on the right things to say and do.

Seph had told Daniel how much she regretted that she had never known him, or her grandmother, Pamela, but her father had enjoyed a happy childhood. She didn't tell him that she had come to know them a little better through Dion, her older, stillborn brother! ...Damn, she shouldn't have thought of him. His first words, when he materialised to her – just as she entered the bar – were of concern that she was okay, and her heart melted.

She felt ashamed that she'd worried about his interfering or teasing her – as she wouldn't be able to hide her emotions from him.

It didn't occur to her that he might help, but it soon became apparent that their grandparents had anticipated that she and Daniel would meet and had told Dion to absent himself unless she invited him. It was lucky that Daniel was distracted, dealing with a waiter, probably making sure they had a good table when they were ready to eat.

Although she and Dion communicated in thought, it wasn't always easy to control her facial expressions or to stop herself from laughing out loud, so she turned away from Daniel, seemingly absorbed by a rather noisy group at the bar. Dion asked if she'd seen the film, 'Angels and Demons', and she hadn't, but said that it didn't sound as if it would be a realistic portrayal of heaven. His grin, as he faded away, indicated that he didn't really care, so she could only hope that he didn't believe everything he saw.

When eventually he caught sight of her, Daniel stood to wave, and walked to meet her, then took her arm to guide her through the not very crowded room... He had managed to look casually smart, even with a tie, so Seph was glad she hadn't over-dressed. Her blue silk suit with a slightly darker blouse was a perfect foil for her silver pendant and earrings.

Daniel pulled out a chair for her, then walked round the table and sat next to her with his back to the wall. Observing the activity in the rest of the bar gave them something to talk about until the bustle of ordering drinks was over, and they were well into nibbling salted roast almonds.

"I see you're a nut-lover too," Daniel smiled, "I foresee trouble ahead. We may even come to blows!"

"You could be right," Seph laughed, hastily grabbing the last of the almonds and rolling her eyes.

Thoroughly relaxed with each other, they observed and speculated about other drinkers at the bar and those sitting around them. A man on a bar-stool, elbows supporting his head, Daniel decided, had been 'stood-up'. Seph argued that his girl-friend had in fact turned up, but they'd had a row and she'd left.

"What makes you think that?" Daniel raised his eyebrows.

"He hasn't looked up once," Seph pointed out, "which means he no longer expects her – so she's been and gone."

Daniel grinned appreciatively and said that she should be the story-teller, not he.

Cocking his head, he gazed at her speculatively and silently acknowledged that despite his doubts about having a personal assistant, he had definitely changed his mind, even before she started work...

They had already chosen from the menu, so didn't have to move to the dining room until they were advised that their food was ready to be served.

All went smoothly. Looking back, three months later, Seph was amazed how many diverse topics they'd covered and by the time Daniel escorted her back to her room, Seph was aware that she felt more in tune with him than with anyone else she'd ever met. She would have to conceal her feelings, otherwise she'd be replaced.

Daniel took her key-card, opened the door for her and handed it back with a warm smile. "Thankyou for a wonderful evening. Sleep well. I'll be going down for breakfast at about nine, but you take your time. We won't be on duty until noon – in reception."

Seph's mind was in a whirl as she prepared for bed. So far so good but meeting his agent would be tricky. The woman might take her appointment as a slight to her own handling of Daniel's relationship to his fans. He would be observing closely how she dealt with the situation – and reporting to his mother no doubt. It didn't cross her mind that he would be wholly on her side.

Snippets of their conversation came back to her and she marvelled again at his way of looking at so many aspects of life was similar to her own. Sleep was slow in coming and morning came too soon.

On the Job

Seph's first thought when she opened her eyes the following morning, half-awake, was worrying about whether the bathroom was free... She needn't have worried about locking his door to the bathroom because the locks worked together automatically. The light over the door was green so, if she wished, she could take her shower early.

Turning over and reaching to the bedside cabinet to check the time on her watch, which she never wore in bed, she couldn't find it. Flapping her hand over the table top, the shock of not finding it jolted her eyes open, and she saw immediately that it was on her wrist!

Good grief ...had she been sober when she came to bed?

Of course, she had.

She always knew when she'd had enough. It wasn't prissy caution that stopped her – it was because whatever she was drinking suddenly tasted foul.

All she could think of after Daniel had said a very formal goodnight to her was how wonderful he was. It was his fault she couldn't think straight. God only knew how she'd keep her mind on the job instead of her boss: she'd have to remind herself of that, constantly!

While preparing for the day and finally donning her grey, tailored suit, she couldn't help day-dreaming; he really had enjoyed her company last night – they had laughed at the same things and he'd sounded sincere when he thanked her as they parted.

Straightening her shoulders firmly, she scolded herself for her stupidity. That was what his fans did, all the time ...worshipped him, and she was supposed to protect him, not add to his discomfort.

In a more sober mood, ready for anything, Seph had gone down to enjoy breakfast, planning, until noon, to wander outside the hotel for a while before reading magazines and watching TV in the lounge.

Her plan worked out, up to the point where

she returned to the hotel after her wandering. Realising that she hadn't handed her card over when she left, she avoided looking at the reception desk, keeping her eyes ahead – until she heard Daniel shouting her name.

He sounded angry, but when she turned to see him leaving the desk, she saw that he looked more worried. "Thank heaven you're alright," he said, gripping her shoulders. Suddenly, pushing her away he apologised. "They told me you were in the hotel and I've looked everywhere in the last few hours."

Seph felt this was an exaggeration but was surprised (and pleased) that he'd worried. When she apologised for her thoughtlessness, he protested, looking a little shamefaced. He was being silly, he admitted; with a wide grin, he then said that he was looking forward to seeing how she handled his agent and her associate.

"You'd better tell me what to expect then," Seph suggested, as they went in search of coffee. "Is she an old dragon or a young one?"

"Not a dragon at all," he replied, "but, I admit, she makes me feel uncomfortable. "Her secretary, or partner – is related but I've never been quite sure what she does – she hardly ever opens her mouth."

Over coffee, Daniel was keen to know what she'd been looking for, out on the street. He made it sound as if she had been up to no good and she was faintly irritated.

She said she was merely interested in the locality and followed up by asking about the bookshop where the signing would take place within hours.

"Don't let's talk about that – tell me about you – what books do you read, for instance..." Seeing her hesitate, looking embarrassed, he added, "I rule mine out, I'd be disappointed if they appealed to you. The first one was produced in a hurry in response to a challenge, but I should never have followed it up with another. I wish I hadn't."

Taken aback by this statement, Seph wasn't quite sure what to say, but couldn't lie. "Your mother gave me a few to read and if you really do want to know what I thought..." Seph held her hand up when he started to protest... "I was impressed by your writing skill. The plots were well thought out and the grammar throughout was impeccable. No editor would have re-worded everything to achieve perfection, so the words must all have been yours."

Daniel looked stunned. "Well, I didn't expect that!"

"You are a talented writer. You could write in any genre, but I don't blame you for being happy enough to keep your very substantial readership."

When he didn't reply, Seph wondered if she had gone too far, but didn't regret having told him. She really believed that his skill was wasted on such a limited market. At that moment the bell-boy approached with Daniel's guests and he stood to greet them.

The agent, introduced as Freda Lipton, was in her mid-thirties, Seph judged, and the younger woman was Joan Lipton. "My niece," gushed Freda. "She's my secretary now, and couldn't wait to meet you again Danny, she adores your books."

Daniel and Seph exchanged looks and, over the shoulders of the two females, Seph mouthed '*Danny*'? After hearing that Seph was Daniel's

PA, Freda looked uncertainly at them both. Seph, ready with her notebook open, smiled and asked a few questions about the venue, starting time, duration of drive.

"You don't need to worry about all that – we'll pick you up at five-thirty. The queue is already forming, by the way, so perhaps we should make it ten minutes earlier." She giggled. "You know how long it takes to get from the kerb to the entrance, don't you Danny?" Seph glanced at Daniel and sensed immediately that the idea didn't thrill him.

She looked sternly at Ms Lipton senior and, in a tone that brooked no argument, informed her, "That won't happen this time. There must be a rear entrance, which we will use with no fuss." While Freda's mouth was still hanging open, she queried, "I can't imagine that you were invited to call Daniel by any other name, so we would prefer that you didn't."

In the silence that followed, Seph wrote notes and Daniel sat back looking slightly bemused. The Liptons looked at each other and the younger one shrugged. It was a *'don't glare at me it's not my fault'* look.

At last Freda found her tongue... "That's ridiculous, the fans expect to see an author arrive and look forward to it."

"I'm sorry, but Daniel is there to sign the books that they will buy inside the store and that's where they will each, individually, meet him. After all," she followed up her point, "Some of the crowd might just be gawpers with no intention of buying. Being jostled outside is more distressing than fun."

Before anyone had a chance to reply, Daniel spoke in support. "That's a very good point, I wish we'd thought of it before, Freda. So Seph and I will take a taxi and see you inside, after you've both greeted the waiting crowd and ushered them in."

Without waiting for their agreement, he suggested that they should look at the lunch menu and went to fetch a couple.

When she'd recovered, Freda asked Seph, "How long have you been with Da – Daniel then?"

In her most sincere tone of voice. Seph informed her, "Long enough to know how happy he is to have you as his agent – he really appreciates your support." Before Freda recovered from her surprise, she said, "Together, I think we'll make an excellent team."

Daniel had returned and was within hearing distance for most of her speech. "I quite agree; couldn't have put it better myself," He smiled as he handed out the menu copies. "Now let's forget work and enjoy lunch."

The food was good, and conversation flowed easily until their guests departed. With a sigh of relief, Seph realised that she was really looking forward to her first book-signing event.

Later when Seph had accompanied him to numerous signings she realised how lucky she had been to sail through that first event so easily. It could have gone so horribly wrong – but it didn't, and it started a trend that, on weekends when there was nothing special happening, Daniel always thought of something they could do together. Once, they even spent a whole two days in Devon, researching the area as a possible scene for his next book!

Showtime

On that first weekend, in Oxford, after lunch with his agent when they were again alone, Daniel told Seph how delighted he was with the way she had taken control of the meeting. "It will be a relief not having to wade through a mob on the way in. I'm sure they are all lovely people individually, but they scare the hell out of me, collectively. Some even grab at my hair – which is no fun, I can tell you!"

He didn't suggest doing anything together but said they should rest until five-o-clock. It was less three hours away, but he had reserved a table for dinner, afterwards, at nine – he hoped she'd not mind his assumption that she would dine with him...! She assured him that she would be pleased to do so and asked what he would like her to wear.

Cocking his head at her, he grinned and said, "Let's see just how glam you can get – the Press might be there." She didn't know how serious he was but decided to dress up and enjoy. As soon as she arrived Seph had unpacked and hung up her clothes. She had a choice of two outfits for every occasion that might arise during their short stay.

Her evening-wear consisted of one full length dress and one mid-calf; she chose the latter, principally, because it had a matching jacket that buttoned up to the neck, suitable for the signing event.

Without the jacket the dress was stunning: form-clinging, with a gentle flare from the hip. The dark cherry-colour suited her and showed off her jewellery to perfection. With everything ready, she set her alarm and lay down to rest. Her growing feelings for Daniel worried her, but she shut out such thoughts and relaxed.

She dwelt instead on all that had gone well, so far – even Dion had not intruded, and she couldn't help hoping that everything was going equally well with him. She was barely conscious of hearing him say something briefly about finding a host for some meeting or other but couldn't make sense of it before her thoughts drifted and she eventually slept.

Seph awoke ten minutes before the alarm was due to sound, so she was able to prepare without rushing.

When Daniel rang to ask if he might call for her – unless she would prefer to follow him down – she was pleased to say she was ready and would like to accompany him. Within a couple of minutes, he was at her door.

The expression on his face, as he took in her appearance from top to toe, was gratifying. "Wow," he drew in a sharp breath. "You always look good, so why should I be surprised. He studied her in silence for a moment – then nodded. "The hair! You have achieved all this without the aid of a salon..."

Seph had swept her hair up into a French pleat, as she often did, without considering it anything special. His reaction was surprising, to say the least. She confined herself to saying that he didn't look so bad himself and they were both smiling wryly as they walked to the lift.

Daniel ordered a taxi at the reception desk. There was no time to sit down before it arrived.

The driver was somewhat surprised when

he was told to find the back door, rather than the front entrance, of the Store, where the signing would take place. Seeing the crowd outside and looking again at the couple in his rear-view mirror, he decided they must be celebrities of some sort and didn't think they'd be happy edging past all the bins and delivery vehicles on the back street, but that was not his problem.

Daniel kept his eyes averted as they drove past the crowd but Seph was fascinated by the way his young fans were behaving. Some were rushing back and forth along the kerb, probably waiting for a Limo to pull up, and others were jostling for places near the still-closed door. A poster on the wall showed a photograph of Daniel. He relaxed and looked back. "To think, I'd have had to battle my way through that throng had it not been for you." He shuddered and suddenly took her hand. "Quite apart from that, I'm enjoying your company and looking forward..."

Having turned off the highway onto a quieter road. the taxi made another turn into a narrow back street and drew to a sudden halt. The driver slid back the privacy window. "Here we are then – sorry I can't get any nearer. The door you want is the green one." The array of bins and discarded empty book boxes seemed formidable, but they reached the door without mishap and it opened after their first knock. Seph had rung ahead to tell them what time they expected to be at the rear of the premises, and all worked well.

Their footsteps echoed as they followed their guide through the rear of the premises, and all was quiet when they reached the shop itself. Freda and Joan were already there, arranging the table and chairs for the signing and placing books within easy reach of the customers. The manager greeted them, smiling happily then glanced at his watch. "Showtime, I think?" Once he was sure that Daniel was ready, he signalled to his assistants to open the doors.

It was almost frightening, the way the crowd surged in, shouting and laughing, each fan eager to be the first to meet Daniel.

Seph had to admire the way the two agents made sure that nobody reached him without first having bought a book!

When they left, a few hours later, it was by the front door. The store manager was delighted to have sold nearly all his stock of Daniel's books, not just the latest book being promoted.

While Daniel signed the remaining few copies, at the manager's request, Freda Lipton joined them, after ushering out the last of the buyers. "I thought the girl in red would never go," she told them. "Three times I saw her off the premises but somehow she kept sneaking back, she even said she needed another book for a friend, but I told her the store was closed."

The manager gave her a sour look and would have admonished her but Seph butted in and said she was quite right; the management and staff had been run off their feet and deserved to shut shop. The manager had the good grace to say that they had done well, and the books would still be there tomorrow, along with more stock. At least they would still have some signed copies, nodding to Daniel who had just finished signing the last one ...and the store wasn't going anywhere!

The store employees, all of whom had worked hard at the tills, managing the queues and running stock back and forth to the signing table, joined them for a well-deserved sip of Champagne, supplied by Daniel, as thanks, before he and Seph departed for dinner.

In the taxi, relaxing happily, they re-lived the highlights of the evening ...like the woman who asked for a short message, to precede Daniel's signature, which he declared was nearly as long as the book!

"You exaggerate," said Seph, "but, the message was beginning to sound as if it was from you personally, so I was glad you clarified that before signing!"

"You were a great help, positioning yourself so that they couldn't crowd me – letting them through one at a time. In past signings, Freda never did anything but talk to them or push open books at me to sign for someone at the back of the queue who had a train to catch!"

He glanced at his watch as the taxi pulled into the kerb, and said, "Good timing. I booked the table for five minutes ago ...so let's enjoy the rest of our evening.

She'd had a moment to think, as they walked inside, Seph recalled Dion's saying they had to find hosts for a party, or was it goats? No ...it was something like hunting goats and that they had to post notes for a meeting! She had been too tired to take it in. With a quick shake of her head she'd dismissed all thought of Dion – she was going to let herself enjoy that night!

It was several days later before she learned anything more about Dion meeting goats at a party...

Hunting Goats?

When Charlie had accepted the fact that his friend Dion really was from the world of spirit and not this one, his mind went into overdrive... Most of his ideas for exploiting this, in order to right the world's wrongs, were to spy on someone or gain information, and entailed Dion going into private property but nothing Charlie said could persuade Dion to break his Gran's instruction about abusing privacy.

Charlie was disappointed and moped for days, but when he saw an advertisement in the local paper inviting interested people to join 'A Ghost Hunting Event', he was immediately fired with enthusiasm. Under the circumstances, he couldn't argue that there are no such things, but he suspected that the hauntings (guaranteed by the poster to be genuine and which all attendees would experience) were not at all real. Someone was operating a scam.

The organisation claimed to have found evidence of ghosts that hunters could witness personally. They said they were equipped with a long list of equipment to record phenomena and those who joined them were never disappointed. It was such a bold claim that Charlie was convinced the evidence was rigged.

Noting the address of the haunted building, he decided to investigate. It turned out to be an old house, which had been a Bed & Breakfast after starting life as a small hotel. According to the notice on the door, it was its reputation for being haunted had led to its closure.

Unable to sell the place, the owner had obviously decided to make money from midnight tours of the haunted rooms. Seeing that it was open to sightseers at two-o-clock in the afternoon, Charlie decided to return after lunch. It only cost a couple of pounds and lasted a mere half-an-hour, unlike the Ghost Hunting tours, which, with all the trimmings, approaching midnight, was nearer to fifty!

While having his pint, with pub food, he concentrated hard on Dion. When he appeared, after an agonising four minutes, Charlie asked,

"Where have you been then? It took you long enough to get here!" With a withering look, Dion disappeared again.

Now, thoroughly upset with himself for being rude, Charlie sought to make amends... "Come back, please, you know I don't really expect you to be at my beck and call, but I'm so anxious to get there before two-o-clock."

"*Get where?*" Dion returned immediately, his curiosity aroused.

Once explanations were over, and they were on their way to *Bide a While* house, Dion became more enthusiastic. Anyone was invited to go inside so there was no problem and who knew? He might see real ghosts ...it could be a fascinating experience.

There was a small queue at the double-doors of the house – enough to fill the few steps that fronted them but not obstructing the pavement. Before joining the end of it, Dion whispered to Charlie, "*Just remember not to talk to me, or they'll think you're mad.*"

"Won't be the first time," Charlie muttered.

"Oh, so you've been here before," commented a woman nearby, turning an interested gaze on him."

"No, no, not to this place," Charlie recovered his poise. "Other haunted places have all been a disappointment."

The doors opened a few minutes later, after Charlie heard that the woman had never been disappointed. She believed she was psychic and was looking forward to tonight's tour. He said he would not be on it and made his way inside as quickly as possible. He saw Dion's wide grin and scowled in response. He wondered if the 'psychic' woman could see him and, if she could, would she know he was a ghost... His thinking was getting muddled; he could hardly ask her! Pulling himself together, he advanced with the queue.

There was no way he was parting with good money to join the nightly hunters himself... He knew he could rely on Dion to relay what was happening. Now, he was observing and guessing where trickery could occur.

The guide, after collecting their entrance fees, told them what night-time visitors had been lucky enough to see and hear. Charlie dismissed ghostly rapping and seriously doubted that there had been a headless woman groping her way down the stairs.

On the way around, Charlie noted several places he needed Dion to check... He was surely right in thinking that tape recorders were hidden in high crannies and shelves – all out of the reach of visitors. He could hardly wait for nightfall and for the ghost hunters to assemble.

Dion noticed several suspicious items behind the scenes. He explored the attic where he found a very impressive switchboard, which, according to the labels, controlled lighting throughout the whole house.

In a small bedroom, on top of a tall wardrobe, there was a collection of puppets; he could imagine how, dangling on their translucent nylon strings, they might throw alarming shadows against walls or curtains, that were already lifting gently, of their own accord, in the draughty rooms. He was more eager than ever to witness the ghostly tour.

Afterwards, when they had exhausted the building, Charlie grabbed a table in the restaurant opposite *Bide a While* and enjoyed a hearty dinner while Dion described his 'finds'. They were both intent on showing up the cheaters – ignoring the fact that a 'real psychic' might see Dion!

The Midnight Hour

Dion wondered what Seph would think thought about their Ghost hunting. If all went well, she was sure to be pleased.

He and Charlie were in a restaurant where Charlie had been for hours and, as midnight approached and the queue opposite the restaurant was disappearing into the haunted house, Charlie urged Dion to go inside and tell him what was happening.

The guide greeted the hopeful hunters, after they had parted with the entrance fee, and explained the importance of keeping as quiet as possible – no distracting others by chatting.

Nipping outside to Charlie, Dion said that the cashier had locked the entrance doors and disappeared up the stairs to the attic. Dion, of course, followed him. Now that the switchboard had an operator, a small screen lit up, showing the expectant group of hunters glancing nervously, but hopefully, into every corner of the dimly lit room.

There were only fourteen hunters in the group. Had there been more, Dion suspected that they would have felt less fearful. They left the reception room at last and entered a corridor that led to a large hall. There were several doors leading off the corridor... All were closed.

"We think something awful must have happened here," whispered their guide. "The air sometimes grows icy cold." The hunters instinctively drew closer together and waited for him to move on, but he stood, with eyes closed and hands together as if in prayer. As he turned, he said, "I was beginning to think we might be spared that tonight, but I think not." Everyone glanced around nervously; the very thought of ghosts really being there was chilling.

In the attic, watching the computer screen over the shoulder of operator, Dion realised that the camera must be sending from inside a small closet. The darkness on the screen was only lit by a crack at the bottom of the closed door, revealing the flash of the guide's torch. The unwitting group outside the concealed closet waited, listening to the guide. The operator flicked a switch on the attic control panel and, in the gloom of the closet, the front of a huge upright freezer swung wide open, nearly touching the closet door. Dion could almost see the gusts of icy cold air falling to the floor and rushing under the door into the corridor.

It was fascinating to see the effect on the hunting party. They stood shivering, partly in fear, until, as one, they moved away to follow the guide, who merely smiled and said he was pleased that they had, after all, shared the experience.

Going to inspect the closet, Dion had to admit it was cleverly set up. A switch clicked the freezer door open and a wooden arm on the wall closed it – operated from the attic, of course.

Catching up with the party, it seemed that they had just been treated to spirit voices, babbling amidst the static hiss and nobody had understood a word of what was said. A scream from a little woman who was hiding her face in her husband's shoulder, turned everyone's attention to her and to where she was pointing. Shadows danced across the ceiling and up the stairs, which led to the bedrooms.

Her husband put his arms around her protectively, declaring that they had seen enough and started to walk back to the corridor. It was an opportunity not to be missed so Dion quickly opened the closet door to reveal the icy freezer and switched the overhead light on, so that it wouldn't be missed.

When Dion described the ensuing chaos to Charlie, they both collapsed with hysterical laughter. Of course, only Charlie's collapse caused any interest. Everyone thought he was ill or having a fit. Brushing off their concern, Charlie hurried outside, to see for himself, how the Ghost Hunters had taken the disappointment of being deceived and cheated.

All wanted their money back! Within minutes the police and press had arrived. Although he hadn't been there, Charlie described for them the various gadgets the pair of crooks had rigged to produce ghostly shadows and sounds and, fortunately, managed to escape without giving his name.

It was a good hour before peace reigned and it was certainly the end of that particular hoax. Charlie realised it was only the tip of the iceberg, but he hoped that hearing and reading about how the 'ghosts' were produced would open eyes to what was, more likely than not, happening in many other places.

Dion returned to *Bide a While* a few hours after it was closed and gradually saw that there really were several ghosts lingering there. None approached him, or even seemed to see him and all went about their everyday tasks, as they must have done when living. He was sad for them – they must be *lost souls* and needed to realise that their lives on earth were over. He would ask if anything could be done to save them. Grandma would know. She knew everything.

Sweet Dreams

Still not asleep, Seph's thoughts were again drifting back to that first weekend in Oxford, by far the most memorable. Their working day was over, and they'd taken a taxi from the book shop to the restaurant where Daniel had booked dinner. They were shown to their table and Seph removed her bolero and hung it over the back of her chair.

Before sitting, she saw Daniel's eyes lingering on her. She could tell that he liked what he saw – not having realised that her outfit was a two-piece. At that moment a young man with a camera dashed up and asked permission to take their photograph!

After he'd taken several, and left, Seph eyed Daniel, deeply suspicious that the incident had been no surprise to him, but he insisted he had only been joking when he spoke of such a thing happening. He had certainly looked surprised, but she'd still had her doubts. It would be interesting to discover where, if at all, it would be published and immediately she wondered what Dion would think of it...

That was a mistake. Dion appeared to her immediately, grinning from ear to ear. Concentrating hard, she impressed on him that she was actually working and would talk to him later. With a slow wink, and again muttering something about goats, he left. Momentarily distracted, Seph forced her attention back to the moment.

It had been a lovely evening. Daniel was attentive and showed an interest in everything she had now discovered about her grandfather and family. She relaxed and found herself on the verge of revealing the source of her information – her lost brother, Dion. She was then suddenly stuck for words. How could she explain her familiarity with a brother who had died before she was born? Daniel voiced his sympathy about her lost grandparents and, realising that she was uncomfortable, changed the subject smoothly. Fortunately, Dion kept his distance for the remainder of the evening.

When they went back to their hotel afterwards, Daniel asked if she had anything planned at home for Sunday? Did she need to be back for any particular time? On hearing that she had nothing in mind, Daniel told her how much he was enjoying her company and suggested they left early for the trip home tomorrow in order to enjoy the drive – stopping wherever and whenever the mood took them.

"You could ring me when you're ready to go down for breakfast and we'll leave straight after. How does that strike you?"

Before admitting that she would look forward to the day out, Seph couldn't resist asking, "I take it that I'm officially off-duty now then?"

"As you have been since the signing finished," laughed Daniel, "and don't pretend you didn't know."

Conversation lapsed as the taxi drew to a halt and they went through the lobby and up in the lift to their floor. At her door, he took her card from her, put it into the lock and pushed it open, but as she walked in, to her surprise, he put a hand on her arm.

"I have to confess that I'm developing quite a crush on you, so if there's no hope for me, you'll have to find a kind way of letting me down lightly... Goodnight."

Turning abruptly, Daniel went to his own door and entered without looking back.

Thoroughly shaken, but happy, Seph moved as if in a dream, preparing for bed. Even after so long a time, she could still recall that moment, as if it were yesterday. She allowed herself to re-live the pressure of his hand on her arm and hear, again, the hope in his voice...

They had come to know each other even better since then, and she couldn't imagine meeting anyone even to compare with Daniel... Perhaps dreams do come true, she sighed happily as she slept at last.

A Day Off

Sunday mornings were normally spent in her room. Her parents sometimes went to church but never commented if she didn't accompany them. After a long lie in, either bed or bath – or both – Seph usually felt ready to face the world. She had the makings of coffee in her room and that was enough – no point in spoiling her lunch! Drifting off to sleep again, she soon found herself dwelling on Daniel and re-living their Sunday drive home.

Coming out of a deep sleep in the hotel, Seph had wondered why she'd set her alarm; why? It was Sunday! Gradually, the thoughts that had sent her to sleep then, seeped back into her mind... Surely that didn't happen... She'd been dreaming.

No, Daniel really had admitted being attracted to her and would be waiting for some indication that she was either tied, or fancy-free. Much as she'd felt like letting her feelings show, she hadn't wanted him to think she was going to fall straight into bed with him, because she wasn't, but it was happening too quickly. Until she knew him better, she'd decided to keep him at arms length. Rumour had it that his name had never been linked romantically to anyone, but unless it was something that stood a chance of being for ever, she hadn't wanted it to start – the let-down would be too devastating.

She remembered wondering then, if he would stay in touch with her during the coming week. Having spoken of his feelings for her, she should have known that he was hardly likely to ignore her for days on end.

When she had rung her parents to tell them she wouldn't be back until late – most likely after dinner – it was difficult to get away without at least saying that all had gone well but, promising to give a detailed account when she returned, she broke the connection and sat back with a sigh of relief.

How could she describe everything that had happened?

Where to start? ...Where to finish!

They wouldn't have been satisfied with a shortened version; they would want to know every detail – especially about her boss!

Leaving her chosen outfit hanging, Seph re-packed her suitcase before hurrying to shower. The novelty of having such an array of oils and shampoo, soaps and such, caused her to spend more time than she'd intended enjoying the endless stream of hot water and she was glad to see that there was a hair-dryer available. Exhausted after all this effort, she had rested for a good half-hour before dressing and thanked goodness she had laid everything out ready to put on before going to wash.

Later, when she opened the door at Daniel's knock, just a few minutes after she'd rung him to say she was ready to go down to breakfast, he caught sight of her luggage, obviously ready to go, and smiled, "Is there no end to your efficiency? How well organised too."

"Please don't bank on it, when I'm off-duty," Seph warned him as they headed for the lift and breakfast.

Daniel's car, had stayed at the hotel while in Oxford, as he preferred to use taxis in an unfamiliar city, so, before collecting it, after they'd eaten, he made sure that there was no shopping she had to do.

Happy that there was nothing to delay them, they took the lift to the underground car park.

Daniel's car was a sporty-looking two-seater. It was comfortable enough but there was something old-fashioned about it. Apparently, it was a classic – a 1936 Singer Leman. Daniel had looked a bit sheepish when he told her that this was his hobby. He loved engineering and there was no challenge in keeping a new car on the road.

Seph thought it was lovely and pleased him by saying that she understood the satisfaction he felt, keeping it smart and roadworthy. She asked if it was difficult to drive and he offered to let her try but when he mentioned double-declutching, she decided that she wouldn't risk it. Her car was a simple gear-change model!

The day turned out differently from her expectations. They didn't visit any monuments or tourist spots.

Daniel turned away from any road that looked busy and they enjoyed quiet country roads. He even stopped when Seph saw a rabbit and waited until it appeared again, lolloping away to hide. The weather was kind to them, warm and sunny, so whenever there was a stunning view or anything interesting to look at, they stopped and walked to look closer.

In one tiny village, they explored the few shops and had coffee at a table outside a café, whose owner had smiled and wished them good-morning. It was invitation enough and a few locals joined them – enjoying new faces and offering advice on anything they wished to know. Eventually they were on the road again.

When they saw a swinging sign outside a public house that looked as if it had been cut out of a story book, Daniel parked and declared it was time for lunch. "The Hungry Man" proved to be all he'd hoped. It was surprisingly full, but the locals moved about, making them welcome and freeing a table and two chairs near the mullioned window, so they could enjoy the view. The food was delicious.

During the afternoon they stopped twice for tea. Daniel excused the second stop by saying it was 'high' tea; the first had been at a place called Lowly Croft! They were within twenty miles of her home at half-past-seven and Seph expected it to be their next stop, but the car pulled into an hotel car park and Daniel declared that, over dinner, they had arrangements to make for next weekend.

He had cunningly left her no excuse for not extending their time together and she wasn't ready to part company yet, so she didn't even try to refuse. After excusing herself to freshen up, she felt Daniel's eyes on her as she walked away and reminded herself that he would probably want an answer to his question before they parted.

The meal was excellent and amazingly, from an extensive menu, they both made the same choices. Daniel couldn't resist pointing out that they seemed to have a lot in common. Conversation flowed easily and next weekend was scarcely mentioned... "Probably in Scotland," he said, "in which case we'll fly up."

As they walked out afterwards, Seph, aware that he hadn't pressed for an answer all day, broached the subject herself.

"In all honesty Daniel, I have to admit that I feel relaxed and comfortable in your company and must thank you for a wonderful day out. In fact, I've enjoyed the whole weekend. There is nobody else I need to consider, at the moment, so I'll be happy to spend time with you."

They had reached the foyer, and seeing his face light up, Seph added, quickly, "I do like you a lot and we can be the best of friends, but I have no intention of committing myself to anyone, exclusively, until I'm convinced it's the real thing."

"For me, this is the real thing," said Daniel, "and until you realise that we are definitely a match made in Heaven, I'm willing to be anything you wish."

"*Escort number one* is as far as I'm willing to go, for the time being," Seph replied, laughing.

"I can live with that," He said, smiling broadly, as he tucked her arm in his and led her to the car.

He opened the passenger door, settled her in the seat and closed it again without another word.

As he took his own seat, started the car and drove it homeward, Seph acknowledged to herself that she could be falling in love with him. There was little point in denying the fact and keeping it from him was going to be difficult, but she had to be sure of his sincerity and that she wasn't just a passing fancy.

He was a rich man, from a wealthy family, even without his notoriety as an author. She needed to be sure that she wasn't being dazzled by his attention, just as much as she needed confirmation that he wasn't being attracted by her resistance, something that was clearly a novelty for him.

When Daniel delivered her to the door after that first weekend away, he waited for her to open it, needing to be sure that she was safely inside – but her parents had heard the key in the lock and rushed to greet her. Daniel had laughed, not at all put out, and they were obviously pleased that he'd waited to meet them.

In some confusion, she managed to introduce him to them and heard him refuse an invitation to stay for hot chocolate... Hot chocolate, good grief. How embarrassing!

Having thoroughly embarrassed her to the point where she hoped the floor would open and swallow her whole, her father picked up her case, carrying it inside and her mother, tactfully, followed him. Daniel give her a quick hug and kissed her cheek ...he would ring her tomorrow, he promised.

Life Goes On

The first thing she noted, as she'd joined them in the sitting room, was that Dion was on the settee. He turned and grinned at her... *"Granddad is pleased with you and Gran is proud that you 'behaved as a young lady should, although sorely tempted... Does that mean you didn't jump into bed with him?"*

Dion seemed to be serious, not making fun of her, so she accepted that he was just confirming what she had taught him. She nodded and smiled as he added, *"We watched Midsomer Murders – it was great."*

To her parents, she said, "So, you've been watching Midsomer Murders..." Seeing their looks of astonishment, she added, "You don't usually."

They looked at each other and then laughed. Each had thought that the other selected the channel.

Dion grinned and faded away. "It sounds as if my brother is settling in well," she smiled. "He looks so happy – I just hope he hasn't been too much of a disturbance."

She need not have worried. They felt that their family was complete again and had loved reading all she'd written that had happened since he reappeared in her life. Dion had joined them again and said he wanted to hear all about her weekend.

"I can't possibly tell you everything tonight," she said aloud for her parents benefit, "but it was most enjoyable, and I love my new job." In answer to Dion's announcement that he would be going with her next time, she replied, "Oh no you won't," then realised that her parents had heard her answer him. They all had a good laugh, when she explained what he'd said, and decided that it was now too late, and they would hear all, tomorrow.

Seph's first thought, when she came around to the sound of early birdsong on Monday morning... was thank goodness she didn't have to be anywhere before mid-afternoon. Her mind, once in gear, kept churning over the past forty-eight hours and she realised that she wouldn't be able to concentrate on anything else until she had satisfied her mother's curiosity.

She was right. What did surprise her was that her father was also at home; he had decided to work in his study today – the office was too noisy. They insisted she had breakfast before they all settled with coffee in the sitting room *'for elevenses'* her mother promised.

Eventually, well into her descriptions of the drive, the hotel and the book-signing, Seph threw in a word about the agent and couldn't resist telling them how she handled the woman and how pleased Daniel was, not having to face the crush of fans.

"It's high time we heard about Daniel," said Jack, earning himself a fierce frown from his wife. "Oh, come on, Jill. You are just as keen as I am to know what he's like."

Seph had to laugh and gave in, admitting that she understood why all his fans adored him – but was being careful not to let him know it. There were things she didn't want to share yet but did say that he'd professed to enjoy her company and had suggested their scenic route home yesterday.

"So, you really like him?" they asked together.

"Yes, thank goodness. He's interesting, a good companion, considerate, a good listener, a perfect gentleman in every way, and he looks stunning in whatever he wears... None of which I will ever tell him – so don't get your hopes up. You're not getting rid of me yet!

The following weekend was more tiring as it meant catching an early flight to Scotland a late one back, and a tiring drive home to Reading in the early hours.

Since then, most weekends had been spent in research. Daniel said they could decide where his next book should be set, and he would value her suggestions for the plot. He made no secret of the fact that he wanted her company and it was obvious that he was still waiting for her to commit herself to a relationship.

Between trips, Seph tried to put him out of

her mind.

A month into her job with Daniel, she was still completing the small weekday jobs she had taken on as a Girl Friday.

This week, her diary was full of dog-walks, baby-sitting and shopping for a man whose wife was away. The husband was alright but his son Frank, who was in his thirties, made her nervous. She wasn't sure why, because he was always pleasant.

She had been attracted to him when they first met, almost a year ago, and disappointed when he hadn't tried to date her. Now that she had Daniel to compare him with, she wondered how she would react to meeting Frank again. It wouldn't happen until Thursday – three days away – so she put these speculations aside and got on with her busy day.

That night, almost too tired to sleep, her thoughts drifted back again, and she remembered worrying about what Dion and Charlie were doing with goats?

In answer to her thoughts Dion had come and told her not to be silly. *"Ghosts, not goats"*.

Hearing how they had succeeded in closing

down the dodgy business venture, Seph was impressed and Dion excitedly told her... *"Look out for Charlie's picture in the news, there were heaps of reporters there, talking to all the angry people."* Seph laughed and said she was proud of him...

Why did her thoughts keep dwelling on her first weekend with Daniel? He had kept in touch between their official duties but been sensible enough not to push for a closer relationship. This was unsettling in one way but comforting in another. Perhaps his patience was beginning to make her feel guilty!

When Thursday did come, she received an email – a lengthy shopping list which took her a good three hours to complete.

Frank was sure to be waiting for her to deliver everything – his father would be at work...

Meeting Frank

It was almost six-o-clock when she rang the doorbell to deliver the shopping and she was surprised to see, when Frank greeted her, that he hadn't changed at all. Her mind flashed back to the impression he had made on her at their first meeting. His good looks and easy, friendly, manner charmed her, and she had quite expected him to flirt with her a little – perhaps ask her out – but he hadn't.

Most men she met 'chanced their arm' by asking ...but perhaps he was already dating, she'd thought. She rarely took such overtures seriously, but in Frank's case she would have accepted; she did, after all, know his family.

As he unpacked the shopping, checking every

item, she suddenly realised why she had been uneasy about meeting him again. He was very much like Daniel! It was not only his looks. He had the same air of self-confidence.

Seph suddenly wondered; if she had spent as much time with him, as she had with Daniel, would she have felt the same about him?

Could she really be so fickle?

When Frank had confirmed that all on the list was there, he asked if the cost had been added to his mother's accounts or had she paid cash for anything.

She hadn't, but as she turned to leave he asked what they owed her for her time.

"Don't worry," she assured him. "Your mother will deal with that."

"The only thing that worries me," he replied, "is that you might get away again, before I work up the nerve to invite you to have dinner with me... How about tonight?"

He looked so nervous that she heard herself agreeing. She almost suggested that tomorrow would be more convenient! Then decided that if she was having second thoughts about Daniel it would better to get her head straight...

Later, as she was preparing for her evening with Frank – deciding what to wear and how to dress her hair – Seph's thoughts were whirling. How had she managed to put herself in this situation? She consoled herself that she had never made any promises to Daniel, and it was only fair to both men to be clear about her feelings.

Earlier, when she'd returned home, she was informed that there was a message from Maggie – she would be needed at the shop again on Saturday. Daniel had probably planned an outing somewhere but would understand that she was duty-bound to help Maggie. He was away with his parents for a couple of days, so she would ring him tomorrow.

Frank was picking her up at eight, so she tried to put Daniel and what he would say about her accepting an invitation to dine with another man, out of her mind.

The restaurant he'd chosen was one she hadn't come across before and the food was fantastic. Frank was very good company and eager to know what she had been doing with herself, while waiting to start her new career in September. She had no hesitation about describing her job with Daniel and Frank said he had a young cousin who adored him and his books; could he tell her about Seph and could she meet the author? When he saw Seph's look of alarm, he laughed and said, "Don't worry, she's not in her teens yet!"

It had been a lovely evening and Seph was tempted to accept Frank's invitation to a show, the following week. When he delivered her to her door later, he shook her hand and said again how much he had enjoyed her company ...no attempt to be any more familiar, so she was glad she had taken the opportunity to get to know him better, but, sweet as he was, he didn't make her breathless, he simply wasn't Daniel.

The following day, Friday, she had an email message from Daniel to say their return was delayed, so he'd ring her tomorrow! She wondered how long the delay would be at that moment that she realised how much she missed him!

She told her father that she might have to leave on Saturday morning before his call came and Jack said, not to worry, he would deal with it.

Seph explained, "I should have given him my mobile number, but I'm not used to this new one yet!"

She was on her way out, opening the front door, leaving her parents to enjoy breakfast when the ringing phone made her hesitate.

"I'll get it," Jack shouted... "It will probably be Daniel." He picked it up and it was, of course. "Seph said you would call ...she'll be glad you've rung this morning as she's due out this afternoon. Yes, I'll pass the 'phone across."

He moved out of the way so that Seph could sit and told her he'd be in his study – it was time he got back to work. Her mother took the hint and moved out with him. They really are the best, she thought.

Now or Never

Daniel first wanted to know where she would be for the rest of the day. When she hesitated and didn't immediately reply, he apologised for being rude and said he hoped they could meet later for dinner, or a show or something.

Seph said she was dog-walking this morning and would be working in the Newsagent's again later, as the owner had another hospital appointment, so she would have to be there to open it up at two-o-clock.

"Fantastic," he said, "I'll come and help, and then we can decide what to do later."

He rang off almost immediately.

Now what?

There was no way Dion would miss being in the shop with her; he enjoyed every minute, but no point in worrying, she would only reveal his presence if she had to. Suddenly, it struck her that even if Daniel, like Charlie, could see him,

Dion would conceal himself effectively unless he was sure that Daniel wouldn't freak out!

When Dion joined her in the car, she seized the opportunity to tell him that Daniel would be coming to the shop this afternoon. Dion looked pleased and, as he faded from her sight, she heard him say, *"Good, that should liven things up."* Not at all sure that it was something to look forward to and making sure she looked fit for whatever lay ahead, Seph went to collect the dogs.

Later, when Seph reached her car, on the way to Maggie's, Dion was waiting for her, snapping himself into the seat belt with a wide grin. He hadn't expected that Daniel would come to the shop and she wondered if she'd been unwise to warn him... Too late!

He glanced at her quickly and said, *"So, we will meet, at last."* Seph was not at all sure that could happen but indicated that she would be mortified if he did anything to embarrass her. With a reproachful look he faded away and the seat belt collapsed.

Seph said aloud, "This is so unfair – you know I enjoy having you there, but he doesn't know anything about you ...that you are back on earth to learn, and even though he thinks he knows me, he might think I'm as mad as a hatter!" After a few minutes Dion returned and asked, *"What are hatters and why are they mad?"*

"Read 'Alice in Wonderland," she said, "It's on my bookshelf." She really should make them aware of each other. It would be better – but how?

To be anything other than honest with Dion would be wrong, so Seph told him that Daniel had said that he loved her, and she hoped he really meant it. Just hearing his voice again had banished all her doubts, but, until she was sure of his feelings for her, she wouldn't admit even that she admired him. Dion was puzzled... *"Why not?"*

"I have to be sure he hasn't said the same to other girls. They all throw themselves at him, so it is possible," Seph told him, hoping he would understand and not interfere in any way.

Although it was not quite opening time, there was a small crowd outside and among them she recognised the 'Freaky Freddy' supporters. She hoped they would still be here when Daniel arrived – they were already eyeing her and muttering behind their hands.

Dion had spotted them and was eavesdropping. *"Freddy is window-shopping at the ironmonger's ...they've sent for him,"* he reported.

Seph was horrified. She doubted that he'd changed and hoped he'd have the good sense to stay away ...but, of course, he might have no idea why they wanted him. Within a few minutes of opening, Freddy walked in and came straight to the counter to buy cigarettes. He waved to the grannies. Seph still didn't know for sure which one was his.

Freddy looked again at Seph and leaned closer... "My, oh my... I had no idea you still lived around here. You look gorgeous, of course. Let's celebrate. Where would you like to go tonight?"

Seph was speechless at the nerve of him, but before she recovered, a nearby stand of books toppled over knocking him to the floor. Daniel had arrived in time to hear what was said but was nowhere near the books.

Afterwards, Daniel said that the way the stand fell was weird. It slid along the floor, upright, before falling. At the time, he'd hurried to Seph's side and put his arms round her, which was the sight Freddy saw when he picked himself up.

One of the grannies (it must have been his) ran to help him up and he glared around to see why the stand had fallen.

"I saw who did it," shouted a little girl, pulling at her mother's hand. "It was him," she said, pointing at a cut-out cardboard model of a pop-star, in front of which Dion was standing. Freddy darted along the isle to sort out his attacker while the child's mother dragged her, screaming, from the shop, with an apologetic smile.

Freddy found that, except for his Gran and her friends, the shop was now empty ...nobody was hiding anywhere near where the child had pointed. He continued to search in a fury for evidence of any attacker and hunted around the display stands until the grannies persuaded him to leave.

His last image was of Daniel and Seph

holding onto each other and glaring at him.

"Well," Daniel whispered, "I hope that will be the last you see of him. I'm glad I was here."

"So am I," said Seph, and, clutching him even tighter in case it was the last time, she took the plunge. "But this seems a perfect time to tell you something that might make you think again before committing yourself further."

He held her away from him, looking earnestly into her eyes for a moment and then held her even closer. "Nothing can stop me loving you – and whatever you tell me will serve to convince me that you consider me trustworthy and there really is a chance that you can love me, and we can spend the rest of our lives together."

Seph almost swooned when he kissed her and fought to regain her composure. She took a deep breath... It was now or never.

Family Ties

Seph's parents were aware that Dion was not with them. They knew that he enjoyed being in the shop with Seph and guessed that he would be teasing any bored children to keep them happy, rendering them less likely to be a nuisance. They also knew that Daniel would be there too and were hoping that all was going well, and they wouldn't clash.

They'd barely had time to settle down after clearing away lunch - Jack sorting files to take to his study and Jill in front of the TV with her embroidery, when they were surprised by a telephone call from Margot Grant. Jill answered the 'phone and mouthed to Jack, *"Daniel's mother."*

It was a long, mostly one-sided conversation.

Jack had no clue what it was about. Jill seemed to be agreeing to something and the more she kept smiling and nodding the more anxious he became. Finally, she repeated a time, seven-thirty, and with a final reassurance that they would look forward to it, she put the 'phone back on its cradle.

"Okay, don't wrap things up," Jack sighed. "What have you let us in for?"

"Margot's family, especially her mother, who remembers your father very well, even affectionately it seems, are anxious that we should all get to know each other. Margot says that they are all happy, and amazed, that Daniel has at last met, and I quote, 'the love of his life'. They say they have never seen him so relaxed and contented."

"So, they assume that Seph is bound to be equally besotted and will one day marry him! Has anyone asked Seph?" Jack frowned and was obviously extremely annoyed, so Jill suggested that they should ask her opinion. Should their acceptance of meeting his family be withdrawn or not?

"Margot is assuming that the young couple would prefer to spend their evening somewhere else but will leave it to them to decide."

After another show of irritation, not having been consulted, Jack admitted that he was looking forward to hearing more about his father's army days. Jill heaved a sigh of relief. It was clear from what Margot had said, that Seph was the first girl to interest Daniel seriously, so at least that was one thing less to worry about.

They couldn't imagine what the young couple would say when they heard of the invitation but decided to invite Daniel to join them for a drink when he called next, either to bring Seph home or take her out. It was difficult to settle down, having so much to think about ...not least was their curiosity about what was happening at the shop.

All was quiet in there now. Earlier, as soon as the doors closed behind Freddy and the grannies, Seph had immediately started picking up books to restore order. She bent down to lift the case back to its feet and, as Daniel rushed to help her, it appeared to float up and right itself. Seph grinned, taking it to mean that Dion approved of her companion and she need not be secretive about him.

Daniel stopped abruptly. "Wow, how did you do that? This stand is heavy enough to need two to lift it – where do you keep your muscle?"

It was a perfect lead to what she had to tell him and a clear indication that Dion wanted his presence to be known, but the door-bell clanged and in walked a customer. To her astonishment it was Shell, who by way of greeting said, "Great – you are on your own, so we can chat." Then she saw Daniel as he stood up with an armful of books. "Oh, I'm sorry, Seph. I spoke too soon."

"No problem, in fact, I'd like to introduce my boss, Daniel Grant. I didn't expect to have to work here today, otherwise I would have rung you." She looked apologetically at Daniel, but having greeted Shell, he said he'd get on tidying the stand.

It was obvious that Shell wanted to know how her new job had worked out, but this was no time to dwell on it or go into detail. It seemed that Shell had tried to ring her at home and been informed that Seph was at the shop. "Your mum didn't tell me you had company – I wouldn't have come – sorry."

It seemed that their usual party of friends were meeting later, and she had wondered if Seph would go with her.

"I'd rather not," Seph said. With a meaningful look, she intimated that she would like to get to know Daniel a little better before she introduced him to the gang, and they already had plans for tonight.

Seph was pleased to note that Shell looked really happy for her, as she whispered... "Enjoy girl – but I'll want a complete update soon."

After Shell left and they were alone again (as far as Daniel knew) Seph said, hesitantly, "I'll understand if what I tell you changes your mind about having anything to do with me..." She stopped him when he attempted to interrupt. "No, hear me out. You might feel too uncomfortable to accept the fact that my brother, Dion, is still with me."

Daniel looked puzzled and looked around the empty shop.

"Before saying more, I'd like you to know that he's sensitive to the fact that he might not always be welcome, and never goes anywhere he is not invited. You saw the book case move ...he was trying to protect me... it is all very complicated..." She paused trying to gauge his reaction – he hadn't backed out of the store – but he did look transfixed. Turning her head a little she realised that, behind her, books were floating off the floor onto the shelves, Dion was clearly trying to show that she wasn't mad...

"I was first aware of him when I was a toddler and he returned to me a few years ago... I would not want to lose him again, before he is ready to move on."

Daniel could see that she was nervous and he could also see, from the evidence floating in the air just behind her, that it was either a very elaborate and pointless trick or she was telling the truth. He asked if anyone else could see him – her parents for instance. "He makes his presence felt," she told him, "ever since they said that they would be pleased for him to come into the house... They told him that he is part of our family and they love to feel that he is with them."

It was a lot for Daniel to take in and he was quiet for several minutes. He had to believe her, he had seen what happened and what Dion had done, surely that was proof. Even so, her heart fell, and her stomach tightened... Would he just leave thinking her mad? Then he looked at her steadily and said, "Dion will one day be my brother-in-law... So, when are we going to be introduced?

Seph sighed with relief. "He'll help you to put all the books back, for a start!" Daniel saw several float from floor to shelf and grinned, as he bent down to restore a few more. He went on to say that he hadn't heard anything yet that would stop him loving Seph.

"Does he wash cars and do laundry?" Daniel asked, and immediately followed this with a loud yell!

Seph couldn't help laughing ...she had seen Dion give Daniel a clip round his ear. So much for worrying about their relationship – it was obvious that they would soon become bosom buddies.

She was even more convinced when Daniel moved several books from where Dion had placed them and told him to take note of the subject matter. Dion had immediately moved a few titles and Daniel said, "Thank you, well done."

Soon after, when order was restored to the shop and the last customers had arrived and left, Seph sorted the counter, locked the inner office and took a last look around the aisles before leaving, in case any customer had inadvertently dropped one of their belongings... She emerged triumphantly with a child's doll and a man's glove, which she labelled with a time and date and put in a box behind the counter. It was already half full of unclaimed items.

Daniel took Seph in his arms and kissed her. "I told you that nothing would change the way I feel... I need you to be part of my life forever."

"Well, you've passed the first hurdle with flying colours," Seph smiled, happily. "Dion pulled a face at us and disappeared... I think we have his approval!"

"Mind you, I didn't expect an invisible brother! I have never believed in ghosts..."

"Oh, for goodness sake don't ever let him hear you calling him a ghost! Ghosts are lost souls who are tied to places they knew in life, which they continue to haunt – probably searching for their loved ones who have passed on."

"Obviously they had more success than the poor ghosts!" Daniel became solemn and said he would remember. The last thing he needed was to offend his new-found, likely-to-be brother-in-law.

They were both in a good mood when they headed for their cars, looking forward to spending the evening together.

Before she realised what he was about to do he had pulled her into his arms and was kissing her, in a gentle, loving way, and she almost swooned. It was as well that he still held her firmly. Looking into her eyes, he whispered... "There, I understand and have sealed it with a kiss."

Seph could still feel the strength of his arms around her and his firm cool lips on hers.

To the Rescue

When Daniel called for her to go out for their dinner date, Seph invited him in to meet her parents properly. She told them that he now knew about Dion and accepted the situation; in fact, he was eager to hear about the many things that had happened, since he appeared to Seph as an adult.

They showed him pictures of Jack in his twenties and Seph said that they could easily be of Dion. It was understood that Dion's presence should be a secret kept by the four of them. Dion showed his approval by swishing the curtains about, much to everyone's amusement.

Daniel and Seph were delighted to hear of his parents' dinner invitation, but preferred to go out, together, on their first official "date", rather than join them. "And Dion can come with us," Daniel said. "In fact, if he wishes, he can choose where we go."

The curtain looked as if someone was swinging on it and Jill told them all to get out, before it fell off."

Outside, Dion headed straight for the passenger seat of the car and was pulling the seat-belt on even before Daniel unlocked the car. Seph grinned and asked Dion if he'd not noticed that the car was a two-seater. Watching, as Dion, with a sigh, climbed into the well at the back, she said, "You'll have to get used to the fact that in this car you are just a piece of luggage!"

As she settled in the passenger seat Seph's face fell. She suddenly realised that Dion had gone. "Come back please, I was joking..." When nothing happened, she repeated, "Come back, please Dion. You're supposed to be choosing where we go." To Daniel, she apologised. "Just start driving. Dion came back to earth to learn, so he's still sensitive and doesn't always know the difference between criticism and teasing. I am really sorry and should be more careful what I say."

Almost immediately, he returned and Seph

greeted him with an apology. Daniel said, "Welcome back. Now tell us where we're going." They were on the edge of town, so he needed to know soon.

Seph was surprised and not pleased to hear that Dion wanted to go to the bar where 'Pug-Ugly' had framed Charlie. When he explained, she understood. They need not stay long but Dion was worried about a boy who had been left sitting outside alone with a drink. He vanished and was back in seconds. *"Yes, he's still there with an empty glass,"* Dion reported.

Having conveyed this to Daniel, they were now heading for the pub, as fast as traffic would allow.

Heavy traffic over the Thames bridge delayed them, making Dion fret, but it cleared on the way into town. On approaching their destination, they were fortunate to find space to park where they had a clear view of the pub and the boy on the bench. who, they decided, was about seven-years-old.

He was restless – Dion guessed he must have been there over an hour.

Daniel was shocked to think it might be the boy's father who'd deserted him. It just wasn't safe to leave a child alone on any street these days, but what could they do? Seph was about to get out of the car and at least offer the child a drink (although Daniel advised against it) when an elderly man approached and sat next to him.

Dion, unseen of course, hovered nearby and reported the conversation. The boy was not inclined to talk at first but when he heard that the man's grandson went to the same school, he relaxed. "His name is Joe, you might know him although he is probably a couple of years younger than you," the man said. The boy shook his head but was now comfortable with the stranger, who had laughed when he had replied that everyone said he was very tall for his age.

"You must be bored, waiting here," the man said. "There are some comics in my car – about to be chucked. If you nip over there and get them from the back seat, you'll have something to read, at least..."

"That's it," said Daniel, getting out of the car. "If he follows the boy to the car I'll go inside and get whoever the idiot is, who left him alone."

"And I'll call the police," Seph declared, getting out and standing by him as they watched.

No sooner had the boy walked halfway to the parked car indicated, than the man stood and hastened after him.

Daniel ran to the pub and entered, looking for the fool who had seen fit to leave the child alone. As he looked around the crowded bar he realised he'd been an idiot, thinking he could single out his target.

He suddenly felt a tug on his arm and was being pushed forward until his arm suddenly rose and clouted someone sitting at the bar. With a roar of anger the man turned but, before he could hit back, Daniel shouted at him. "Your little boy, outside... Quick, get out there, he's being abducted!"

There was no sign of man, boy or car, when they reached the kerb. And Daniel had a hard job calming him down. "My friends will know where they are, and we've called the police. Just sit down for a minute."

It was, in fact, only four minutes before a police car arrived, and the constable, who introduced himself as Jennings, was pleased to have two witnesses who also seemed confident that they could help him to find the boy. He stared hard at Seph and his eyes widened. "You are the young lady who helped us to put a murderer away, aren't you? Is catching criminals a hobby of yours?"

While Seph was deciding how to answer, Daniel said, "These days everyone should be vigilant. Despite the best efforts of our police force, there just aren't enough of you to see everything." His smile took the edge off his comment, but it encouraged the man to concentrate on the crime in progress, as intended.

Seph told Daniel that the abductor had driven through Reading and was now crossing the river, so they should follow.

Jennings was mystified. The young woman appeared to be in radio contact with someone already following, but he couldn't see any wires. Seeing this, Daniel muttered, "Telepathy," and, jumping into his own car, where Seph was already buckling herself in, told Jennings to follow them.

After they crossed back over the river and were well on the way to Wallingford, Seph said they should slow down and look for a tree-lined road on their right. It's a few yards beyond a blue-painted gate, she told Daniel. Turning into the road, they were now looking for house number twenty. It was no problem as the abductor's dark green car was in the drive.

Parking, before reaching the house, Daniel walked back to tell Jennings. Together, they walked to the house and noted that the car bonnet was still warm. Indicating to Daniel that they should retreat, Constable Jennings then made contact with his HQ and whispered, "There's a station a quarter mile away, so back-up should be here within minutes. It's unlikely that the man will put up a fight, but we can't risk frightening the child more than he already is."

Seph had stepped out of the car and was watching but hanging back, so Jennings walked over and asked where her informant was. Hearing that he had gone and didn't wish to be involved, Jennings had to accept that he would never know.

After the back-up police arrived, everything happened speedily. When the door-bell wasn't answered, and screams were heard from inside, the door was forced open and the police went in. Within seconds the child was brought outside, Seph and Daniel rushed to his side. Even though they were strangers he clung to them and Seph cradled him in her arms as he sobbed. Eventually, he looked up at her and pushed away slightly. "I'm sorry," he said, "I'm not usually such a baby, but my dad will kill me for getting conned by that old man."

Daniel looked solemn. "Does he often leave you alone when he goes for a drink?" The boy nodded, and Daniel shook his head. Somehow, he'd make sure it never happened again. "Well, I'm Daniel and this is Seph. We are your friends now and we'll give you a phone number to ring if you're ever scared."

"I'm Jimmy, and I'd like that. Thank you." He stared at Daniel, then shrieked with delight. "You're that writer, aren't you? My sister has all your books. She's going to marry you, she says – is that right? Wow, she won't believe I've met you!"

Daniel frowned and said, "You've mistaken me for someone else..." Putting his arm round Seph he added, "This is the young lady I intend to marry."

Jimmy gave him a disbelieving look... "You sure look like the picture on all the book covers."

It took half an hour to make their statements at the Police Station and, as they left, they saw Jimmy's father, still being questioned. "He'll probably be charged with neglect, Jennings said happily, and they could only agree that he should be.

Back in the driving seat, Daniel asked if Dion was still with them. "He did really well – it's a pity he can't enjoy a meal with us." Daniel felt a tug on his seat-belt and smiled. "I gather he is..."

Seph laughed. "He's very happy that you've accepted him so readily, but is now going to see his friend, Charlie. He's the only other person who can see and talk to him and the poor man didn't know that for weeks. He didn't seem to notice people giving him a wide berth, suspecting his sanity as he waved his arms and chatted to Dion. I had to meet him to explain. Now, they dream up all sorts of ways to save the good and catch the bad."

"Perhaps we could help," Daniel suggested, "Let's go and find them."

"I don't think that would be a good idea," she replied, "but we could ask Dion if there is any way we could, without telling Charlie. I think he likes feeling that he is Dion's only friend on earth."

It was no surprise to Seph that Dion instantly returned to them and declared it to be a great idea, but only if they didn't tell Charlie!

The End of a Perfect Day

Jill and Jack were tired, but happy, after returning home from their evening with Daniel's family. The younger members had been there to greet them and chatted for an hour or so but didn't stay for dinner.

"I wondered why we'd been invited so early," said Jill, "but it was nice to meet them. Daniel's grandmother wouldn't have been able to tell you so much about Martin, your father, had they stayed to eat."

"It was wonderful. I feel I know him better now than I ever did. He never spoke much about his service life. She was obviously fond of him and felt safe with him because he was engaged to a girl back home – my mother of course..."

"It was really interesting looking through her photograph albums," Jill commented. "Your father was almost as handsome as you are – I expect there were a good many you've never seen."

"That's true," agreed Jack. "I mean, about not having seen many of them, not my being more handsome! My father must have had similar snaps; perhaps they're packed away in the attic. – I'll have to look one day."

"As if you ever have time!" Jill grinned.

At just before midnight they heard Seph's key in the lock. She wasn't surprised to find them still up – probably just waiting to hear that she had enjoyed her evening. They were astounded when Seph flopped into a chair and launched into an account of their amazing adventure; boy at risk, the abductor chased, police involvement and father likely to be prosecuted.

"It was Dion who saw the boy first, all alone outside a bar with an empty glass and, thank goodness, we went to investigate. When we eventually got around to eating, Dion didn't stay but I'm relieved to say that they have accepted each other without hesitation."

Realising that she hadn't asked about their evening, Seph remedied that by asking... "Did your dinner date go well?"

It had obviously gone extremely well, and they now knew Daniel's family far better than she did... The thought pleased Seph.

Hearing about the collection of photos that might very well be in the attic, Dion suddenly returned and volunteered to ask his granddad where they might be. They finally went to bed, happy that things were going so well. Jill and Jack were filled with joy that even if they couldn't see him, their first-born child was restored to them. They understood that he was unlikely to be with them forever but took solace from what they had already received.

Before slipping into bed Seph peered through the bedroom window and, as expected, she saw Dion sitting near the rockery, smiling. He waved, and she heard him say, *"If you thought today was fun ...just wait for tomorrow!"*

With such a threat hanging over her

head – how could she possibly sleep?

If anything, though, it wasn't his remark that kept her awake, it was re-living the evening she had spent with Daniel. They had eaten at a restaurant neither had tried before and enjoyed the food so much that it was bound to become one of their favourites. I would have enjoyed being anywhere with you," smiled Daniel, "but we'll certainly come back to this place." They each revealed more about their past to each other; where they had lived, their adventures and misadventures at school and with friends. They couldn't hear enough and would have talked all night, had they not suddenly realised that the restaurant had emptied of diners, and their waiter was hovering – albeit at a distance!

The following day was likely to be busy for them both, so they decided to keep in touch by 'phone. She expected they would have to attend another book-signing on the coming weekend... Her life was suddenly a whirl of activity and she found it difficult to switch off and sleep. At last, she did drift off and was soon dreaming – of Daniel, of course.

A Lucky Escape

After leaving Seph and Daniel earlier that evening, Dion had joined Charlie on a bench outside yet another public house in town. Whether Charlie knew it or not, Dion couldn't guess, but it was where Seph achieved local fame by unmasking a murderer...

At Dion's approach, Charlie had startled two young women by (apparently) greeting them warmly and asking where the hell they'd been. Dion, who, of course, was invisible to them, hurried to Charlie's side, redirecting his gaze, and they rushed into the pub, giving the bench a wide berth. Charlie was too busy telling Dion about the big drug deal that was going down to protest!

The house opposite was his target, and Dion was shocked when he realised that it was where Seph's friends lived on the top floor... More to the point, her friend Shell had said there was a party there tonight. It was difficult, verging on impossible to make sense of Charlie's reasoning. He'd seen a shady-looking character handing a suspicious package to a guy who looked guiltily over his shoulder before parting with a fistful of notes. *"Is that all?"* Dion asked. *"It could have been anything. I know there's a perfectly respectable party there tonight, on the top floor, and all the other tenants are elderly folk, unlikely to be drugees!"*

Dion went to check inside the building then returned to inform Charlie...

"The hosts learned that one of their guests had a birthday today and sent out for a gift – and it was definitely not drugs!"

Charlie shrugged. He was disappointed. So, what would be their mission for tonight then?

Dion suggested that he just enjoyed his drink and cut down on the chat, because several people were giving him funny looks. *"You may well get thrown out if they think you're already drunk!"*

Three hours later, Charlie really was drunk, but no longer unhappy. Dion walked beside him as he staggered home, which was just as well. A car came speeding round a bend as Charlie started to cross the road and Dion managed to hurl him back onto the pavement... The car tyres screeched as the brakes were slammed on.

The driver climbed shakily from his seat to make sure that Charlie was alright. "If I hadn't seen it with own eyes," he said, "I'd never have believed anyone could jump so far, so fast. Thank God you're fit."

Charlie had, unsurprisingly, not landed on his feet and would undoubtedly be bruised but, slowly coming around, he realised how lucky he'd been and thanked the driver for caring. The man drove away at last – a lot more slowly than he had arrived.

As he reached home, Charlie became maudlin and with tears in his eyes kept thanking Dion for saving his life. It was an hour later before he tumbled into bed and Dion finally felt it was safe to leave him. He knew it was too late to visit Seph, so he spent a few hours in Singapore and watched a film in New York. It was about a man who talked to a young boy who had died and passed over, but the man didn't know.

He enjoyed the film but was more amused by the comments made by the audience on the way out. One woman, who declared it to be rubbish and too far-fetched for her, made him laugh and he laughed even more when she looked straight at him and said, "Is there something about me that you find funny?... How rude," she added as she turned away.

When he eventually returned to the rockery, it was daylight and he saw movement inside the house. Jack was in the kitchen. It gave him an idea. Remembering the photographs, he 'messaged' his grandfather and asked if any were hidden away in the house... Smiling, he eventually joined his father and, hearing the curtain swishing, Jack greeted him with a wave and smile.

Jill arrived and Seph followed just as the kettle boiled and it was clear to her that Dion was bursting to tell them something... "Right-o," she said, turning away from her parents. "Now, what are you so happy about?" After listening for a few minutes, she smiled and turned to face them again. "Come with me…"

Walking out of the kitchen, down the long hallway, she stopped outside the sitting-room door. They thought she was going in but, instead, she turned towards the stair wall and removed the picture that hung there. To their surprise, she handed it to Jack and turned her attention to the hook. As she turned it sideways something clicked, and a door swung open to reveal several deep shelves.

They were astonished, realising that this was at the end of the under-stair cupboard, where they stored an assortment of nondescript things. They had never suspected that another cupboard was at the end of it – a secret hidey-hole! In addition to several old photograph albums there were a few small boxes, in which they found letters, legal documents and jewellery.

It was exciting but extremely upsetting to think that they might one day have sold the house, never having known of the existence of these personal and treasured items belonging to Martin and Pamela. Clutching the albums, Jack said, "Thankyou son and please thank my father." He took them to his study and, with tears in his eyes, settled in his favourite chair to go through them.

Dion was happy – he'd done two good deeds in one night and his grandparents were pleased with him. He had wondered how it had been possible for him to lift Charlie as he had, and Grandma smiled. She said that being so close to Seph and his family had built up his confidence. When he suddenly needed it, his adrenalin had kicked in and given him strength.

Gran was right again, but when he tried now, several times, to move several heavy objects, he had no luck at all. With a sigh, he realised that he should be checking on Charlie. When he eventually described his adventure to Seph, he needed to be able to say that it had ended well.

Another Night Out

It was difficult to believe they had known each other for less than a year. They'd slipped quickly into a regular routine. Seph's mornings were busy: shopping for a man whose wife was in hospital, occasional shop-sitting and walking dogs. The afternoons were easier, as she had only to do some household chores for a woman who had broken her arm. Monitoring Dion's education was a continuing joy and the weekends took care of themselves, with Daniel, whether there were signings or not.

A year to the day, after their first proper date, she wondered if it would be silly to celebrate it, but, just in case, she headed home after her last job, as quickly as she could, in case Daniel phoned.

It was fortunate that she was home early, as her father rang to ask if she could stay with the senior Mrs Mather again, straight away. Her son and his wife had been called away, urgently. They needed Seph to be there at six-o-clock or as soon as possible after – in which case, his mother would be delighted to let her in. A glance at the clock told Seph she could be ready to leave quite easily, to be there by six, so he could tell Mr Mather not to worry.

Daniel had rung earlier to say that the weekend signing had been postponed – both agents were ill, so the venue had not been confirmed and they would have to choose another date. He suggested that they had a night out – take in a film perhaps? "As long as it isn't about heaven," said Seph. "If it is, I'll have Dion chattering about it non-stop!" She then wished she hadn't said something that sounded like criticism... Fortunately, Dion wasn't with her.

Now she had to ring Daniel to say she was Granny-sitting, again. He was disappointed but, when she said that the son and his wife should be home between nine-thirty and ten, he decided, in that case, that he would drive her there and collect her later – no need for her to take her own car. Although this sounded dictatorial, he did wait for her to agree before ringing off, with a final, "On my way then!"

As the car pulled into the driveway, Seph saw the sitting-room curtain open and Grace waving to greet her. The front door opened at the same time, and her son emerged with his wife, smiling. Seph waved goodbye to Daniel and, while her husband went to fetch his car, Mrs Mather thanked Seph for coming.

Eyeing Daniel's departure, she hoped they hadn't ruined her evening. She also apologised for not having prepared dinner for them, it had been such short notice. "There's salad and other cold stuff in the fridge – I hope that's alright?"

Seph assured her that it would be no problem and went to join Grace. After the bustle of goodbyes and making sure Seph had their mobile numbers in case of emergency, peace reigned at last.

With a sigh of relief, Grace settled into her armchair and demanded to know what Seph had been 'up to' since her last visit.

It was so long ago, Seph thought ...and so much had happened. The first significant thing she could think of was joining the book circle, so she mentioned that her friend Shell was helping one of the older members by editing and proofreading her autobiography.

"Who's that then? Would I know her?" Grace demanded."

After a moment's concentration, Seph recalled, "Letty Ledbetter," and Grace laughed.

"Oh, no... Not the cat woman!"

Seph confirmed that it was and wished she could have related the story of their afternoon with her. She couldn't, of course. Even Shell didn't know how the stuffed cat came to be sitting in a tree!

She wasn't going to say anything about the murder opposite the shop and helping the police either, but Grace forestalled her. She had read the newspaper account and been very impressed.

Seph was embarrassed, as she hadn't been the clever one and hurried on. *'Becoming PA to a writer'* was not enough information for Grace, who eventually pushed her into giving his name.

"Daniel Grant... Yes, I know his books – bought every one of them for my teenage granddaughter – she loves them." After several times tapping her head, Grace said, "His grandmother is Tricia Millais. I have all her books too."

Surprised, Seph couldn't help asking if she might borrow one to read as she hadn't been able to buy them; they were out of print. "Of course, dear, borrow them all." After a thoughtful moment she said, "Having seen you arrive in a strange car, I asked if that was your young man and you said 'yes'. It was Daniel wasn't it?" When Seph nodded, she wanted to know if the relationship was serious. Seph had to admit that it was, not guessing what was coming next! "So, I've ruined your evening. I'm very sorry and there's only one solution to that. Call him now and invite him to dine with us."

Grace would brook no argument and picked

up the house phone. Seph realised that she was ordering a takeaway when Grace asked if Chinese was alright? She used her mobile to call Daniel and he was delighted. Repeating his words to Grace, Seph added that it was very kind of her, and Grace's reply opened the door for Dion as well! "Any friend of yours is welcome here my dear," she said.

The party that followed the introductions, was nowhere near as riotous as the last, but even more fun for Seph. She couldn't stop Dion from telling her what the other two were holding whether in scrabble or poker! Daniel guessed and thought it was hilarious. He couldn't stop grinning. Grace couldn't get over how clever Seph was, and said, "I'm glad we're not playing for real money!"

Dinner was a huge success too and Daniel helped Seph to clear away and clean up afterwards.

Like her father, he chose to wash rather than dry the dishes and at last the kitchen was restored to order. As they were about to rejoin Grace, Daniel turned to face her with an anxious look in his eyes. Before she realised what he was about to do, he had pulled her into his arms and was kissing her, in a gentle, loving way, and she almost swooned. It was as well that he still held her firmly.

To her astonishment he took a small box from his pocket. Opening it and offering her a beautiful diamond ring, he asked her solemnly, "Darling Seph, please, will you marry me?"

He started to fall to his knees, but she pulled him up and whispered that she would. He placed the ring on her finger and kissed her again.

Looking into her eyes, he whispered... "Thank you my darling. I will do my utmost to make you happy."

Whenever she recalled that moment Seph could still feel the strength of his arms around her and his firm cool lips on hers.

Tearing herself away at last, Seph said they should get back to Grace. "Let's tell her," she said. "She really is a dear and she'll be thrilled to be the first to know."

Seph was right. Grace cried with happiness and hugged them both. After admiring the ring, she excused herself for a few minutes and returned holding a bottle of champagne.

Perhaps it was fortunate that her son and the *'real Mrs, M'* returned, soon after the bottle was opened, as they were able to help empty it and Daniel didn't have to worry about driving Seph home. He had intended finding somewhere romantic to 'pop the question' but he hadn't been able to wait. Now it seemed only fair to face her parents – though it might be a bit late to ask for her father's approval.

It was just after eleven-o-clock when they let themselves into the house and went to join her parents in the sitting room. Seph was pleased to see that Dion was with them. While greeting her mother, Seph saw her father stand up and leave the room with Daniel. Within seconds, they returned, both smiling broadly, so Seph held out her hand to show Jill her ring. Soon they were all standing in a group hug.

Neither Seph nor Daniel revealed that it was the second bottle of champagne they had seen opened that night... It had certainly been a night to remember.

In the Beginning

It was the early hours of the morning, before Daniel left and an hour later before her parents were willing to stop talking and allow her to go to bed.

"I understand from Daniel that he hopes the wedding will be soon rather than later," Jack said to Jill, "so we'd better start saving up!" Laughing, he told Seph, "He's planning to take you house-hunting tomorrow, by the way. Did you know?"

Seph was surprised, but quite excited.

"I'm not sure I'll be up to it," she said. "It has been quite a hectic night! Now I understand what people mean by a whirlwind romance!"

Jill wanted to know how Dion felt about her engagement and, as she was sitting on the settee, she had the answer, immediately, and started laughing. "Someone is jumping with joy at the other end of this sofa,"

"He was there when Daniel proposed," Seph told them. "In fact, he saw it coming and before Daniel spoke to me, he left us and went back to Grace. You should be proud of him; he is so sensitive. Now, before his head starts swelling, I'm off to bed!"

Before they went the rounds of every estate agent within reach, on Saturday morning, Daniel took her to meet his family again. They all wanted to tell her how pleased they were, that he was being taken off their hands at last, according to Daniel...!

As he turned into the driveway, Daniel said, "Please let Dion know that he is always welcome to come with me, wherever I am, including this place."

"You'd better not cheat on me then," was Seph's immediate retort; "He's nodding happily, by the way."

It was such a relief that they accepted each other so readily – she even wondered if they'd ever gang on her! Dion was still grinning as they went inside, where they were all waiting – brothers, sisters – both still holding their cell phones - parents and of course Grandma, who was openly moved to tears. It had, of course been her idea to bring the pair together.

The brothers' wives were both at work. Perhaps it was just as well, because the father of the soon-to-be groom insisted on taking everyone out for lunch, and even rang her parents and invited them too. The presence of another two would have made thirteen at the table,

It was far too late to call on any agents by the time the party broke up, so Daniel and Seph went to watch the film they had missed last night.

Later, after they had enjoyed their evening and were on the way home in the car, Daniel asked if Dion had enjoyed the film. He had, Seph told him... "He's now gone off to see if there are still cowboys in the Wild West. He asked me where it is, but my geography isn't up to much. I told him to follow the signs to Texas."

"It probably isn't as wild as it was, so he might be disappointed." Speaking of Dion, Daniel wanted to hear more about their first meeting, when she was just a toddler. He asked her how much she could remember about Dion as they were both so young...

"Well, I didn't know his name. I was, as you know, about three-years-old. We hadn't been living in the house long enough for my mother to make friends with other mothers and their families, so I played on my own in the garden, every day. I had toys of course but I must say I was lonely. My mother kept a close eye on me and often came out with treats to share but, not surprisingly, I wasn't really happy ...and was always delighted when somebody came."

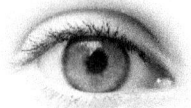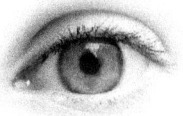

by Mai Griffin

Ghostly Echoes Series

Ghostly Echoes
A Poisonous Echo
Dangerous Echoes
Haunting Echoes
Restless Echoes

Stand Alone Fiction

Somebody Came

Short Stories

Picked and Mixed
Anthology

As an Illustrator

Donnington's Reef
Various publications for
Dorchester Abbey, Oxon

For her paintings

www.maigriffin.com

You can find Mai's books on Amazon, Kindle, iBooks and Kobo.
They can be ordered through all major booksellers, worldwide, and
from the publisher's website www.uppbooks.com